Darcy's Secret Marriage

By Zoe Burton

Darcy's Secret Marriage

Zoe Burton

Published by Zoe Burton

© 2019 Zoe Burton

Early drafts of this story were written and posted on fan fiction forums in April 2019.

ISBN-13: 978-1095556702

Acknowledgements

First, I thank Jesus Christ, my Savior and Guide, without whom this story would not have been told. Thank you for growing me in You. I love you!

Additional thanks go to my betas, Heleen, Christa, and Kristie. Thank you for your hard work and encouragement.

A *huge* thank you goes to my friends Leenie and Rose, who always have my back.

Finally, this book was written for my patrons at Patreon. Angela, Barbara, Cheryl, Christa, Debbie, Doris, Gail, Joan, Kimberley, Leenie, Lisa, Marsha, Peggy, and Rose, your support awes and humbles me. Thank you! <3

Table of Contents

Prologue

June 26, 1810

I cannot fathom it, but Elizabeth Bennet is here, in Scotland, and staying with a local couple on their estate just a few miles away. What is alarming is that my son knows and is all but courting her. He is sly and will not speak about it to me, but I hear from the neighbors things he will not say.

I must get rid of her! I do not have the connections here that I do in Derbyshire and London, but surely someone can be found to undertake this task. It will have to be completed by the hand of another. My previous methods were effective, but the recipients were all members of my own household. The Bennet chit is not here at Glenmoor.

No matter how difficult I find the task, this girl will cease to be a distraction to my son. He <u>will</u> marry where I wish him to. I always win.

Chapter 1

Early summer, 1806

Twenty-year-old Fitzwilliam Darcy raced his stallion, Apollo, across the fields of Pemberley. Though he was exhilarated by the rush of wind and feel of the horse's movement underneath his seat, his heart pounded in anticipation; he was on his way to meet his love, his Elizabeth. They had taken to walking together every morning, sometimes with his sister or cousins, sometimes with her eldest sister, and sometimes alone. He cherished this time with her and knew she felt the same.

A few minutes later, he slowed the animal down to a canter. He was approaching the turnoff to Lambton, and Apollo needed to cool down a bit, anyway. Looking around, Darcy searched for Elizabeth. He slowed the horse down further, to a trot and then a walk, his eyes darting to and fro. Just as a crease began to form between his brows, he saw her, alone, wandering up the road toward him, stopping now and then to sniff a flower or observe a bee. Pulling his steed to a stop a few feet away from her, Darcy dismounted and waited for her to approach, his gaze wandering over her form, from the chestnut curls peeping out from under her bonnet to her black half-boots, dusty from the mile-long walk from her aunt's house.

Miss Elizabeth Bennet was visiting Mrs. Penelope Hayes at a neighboring estate, Rocky Hills, and had been in residence for the last six weeks. Darcy had been instantly smitten with the always-smiling, witty young lady of six and ten. That she returned his feelings delighted him, and the two had, over the course of time, fallen deeply in love.

The Darcys were close neighbours with the Hayes family, their estates bordering each other, and were frequently in company together. As a result, Darcy and Elizabeth had spent much time together. They had discovered many similarities between them, and not a few differences. They had even clashed a few times, much to the dismay of their companions. Though he had known Elizabeth but a few weeks, Darcy knew he would propose.

There was only one problem: his mother. Though his father, Mr. George Darcy, was delighted with Elizabeth, Lady Anne Darcy was not so pleased. She wanted Darcy to marry her niece and namesake, Anne De Bourgh, but her husband had refused to allow her to arrange that marriage. Lady Anne was angry about his decision. She decided that, if her son were not permitted to marry his cousin, then he would marry a girl with a title and a huge fortune. Elizabeth Bennet had neither.

The couple fought over it many times that summer, with Lady Anne demanding that her son be sent away. Eventually, Mr. Darcy reluctantly gave in, arranging not only a tour of the kingdom for Fitzwilliam, but also a stay beforehand in London with a friend of the family. Darcy and Elizabeth were suddenly torn apart, with no knowledge of where the other was.

Scotland, four years later

Fitzwilliam Darcy had arrived at his family's Scottish estate, called Glenmoor, a week ago and had promptly received an invitation to a ball from his gregarious neighbor, Mr. Brodie, to be held at that gentleman's estate, Bonnyvale. Darcy did not enjoy balls, but he knew what was expected of him, and so agreed to attend.

Standing off to the side and away from the dancers, Darcy observed his fellow attendees. His host approached, and Darcy turned his attention to the red-haired gentleman.

"Mr. Darcy, so good of you to come! I was sorry to hear about your father; he was a good man."

"Thank you, sir. It was a shock, but we are managing." Darcy felt his heart squeeze in pain. He missed his father terribly.

"How long has it been now?" Brodie lifted his glass of punch to take a sip.

"Three years. I was halfway through my tour when it happened. By the time a letter reached me and I made it home, the funeral was over. My mother was devastated."

"How is your mother? My wife and I have not seen her in years, but I remember that she was a beautiful and elegant woman."

"Thank you." Darcy lifted his lips in a small smile. "She remains much as she has always been. She is over the worst of her grief, I believe."

"Good, good. I think to call ladies the weaker sex is a mistake. They are able to bear far more than we mere gentlemen can." Brodie clapped Darcy on the shoulder. "You have turned into a fine man, Fitzwilliam Darcy. I look forward to getting to know you better during your stay." He gestured toward the room with the hand holding his glass. "I must go and greet more guests. Get out there and dance, will you? You are too young to hide along the wall." Laughing, Brodie shook Darcy's hand and wandered away.

Darcy looked down, shaking his head and grinning. Mr. Brodie had always been one to speak his mind. After taking another sip of punch, he looked around the crowded ballroom, examining every face. It was a habit he had gotten into four years ago, when he was unceremoniously ripped away from the love of his life and sent on his tour. At this point, he did it without thought. His attention was suddenly arrested by something on the far side of the ballroom.

Could it be? Darcy was certain it was. Suddenly, the crowd parted and there, on the other side of the room was Elizabeth Bennet.

~~~***~~~

Elizabeth stood beside her aunt, Maddie Gardiner, as she observed the dancers. Her party had been the last to arrive at the ball, and she had not yet been asked to dance.

Elizabeth and her aunt and uncle were in Scotland on a leisure trip, though her uncle, Edward Gardiner, was using part of the trip for business purposes. They were guests of one of Gardiner's investors, a Mr. Gerald Reid, and were staying at his estate nearby.

Maddie shook her head as she saw Elizabeth rise up on her toes to examine the guests. "Do you still do that? Search crowds? It has been a long time."

Elizabeth dropped back to her heels, turning to face her aunt. "I do still look. And, yes, it has been a long time." Elizabeth felt her face turn red and her body begin to burn. She opened her fan and waved it to cool herself off as her eyes began to search again.

Maddie did not speak for a moment, a small crease forming between her brows as she examined her niece. Finally, she asked,

"You have never told me for whom you are looking. Is it someone in particular?"

Elizabeth sighed. She had not told her aunt of her lost love. Only her sister Jane really knew how she had felt that long ago summer when she had fallen madly in love. Though she trusted her aunt, the pain of her disappointment was still sharp after all this time. She moved her gaze from the dancers to meet Maddie's.

"Yes, there is a specific person for whom I search." Elizabeth was hesitant to say more, for fear of being rude, but she needed her aunt to understand that she did not wish to speak of it, at least not here and now. Drawing a deep breath and letting it out in a soft sigh, she added, "I ... cannot ... at present tell you who it is." Her lips quirked up in a flash of a smile. "Perhaps one day I will be able to speak of it to you."

Maddie examined Elizabeth once more, but said nothing beyond, "Very well." She gave her niece a reassuring smile and then watched as Elizabeth's eyes moved back toward the dance floor.

Elizabeth was relieved that Maddie had left off so easily. She suspected that there would be more questions at a later date, but that would work in her favor, for it gave her time to compose her responses and her emotions.

The end of the set of dances arrived, and the music stopped. As the crowd departed the dance floor in favor of refreshments and conversation, Elizabeth's heart stopped as she recognized a gentleman on the other side of the room. "Fitzwilliam," she whispered. Her attention riveted to the man across the way, she froze, willing him to come near.

Darcy knew the moment Elizabeth recognized him by the way her whole face lit up, a smile entirely covering its lower half. He began to move toward her, an answering grin spreading over his own mien. He skirted around a couple who stopped in front of him, impeding his progress, but paid them no mind. Finally, he was there, standing in front of her. He bowed.

"Miss Bennet, how are you?" *I have missed you, you are beautiful, I love you.*

Elizabeth blushed even as her smile grew. She curtseyed gracefully, saying, "I am well, Mr. Darcy. How are you?" *Oh, how much more handsome you are! I did not know it was possible. I love you so!*

"I am well." Darcy tried to assume the indifferent mask that was considered proper by high society, but he could not. Not after finding his Elizabeth after all this time. Hearing the musicians strike a chord, he asked for the next dance.

"I have this set free; I would love to dance with you. Thank you." Elizabeth tucked her hand under the elbow Darcy held out and felt again the shot of lightning straight to her heart that touching him had always inspired.

Darcy forced his free hand to his side, clenching his fist. He wished more than anything at that moment to lay it over Elizabeth's where it rested on his arm, and to entwine their fingers in the same manner their hearts had been so long ago and, he hoped, still were. Looking down at her, he recognized the same look she had worn the last time he saw her and knew he had reason to hope. *If not for all these people staring at us, I would whisk her to the corner and talk to her. Find out if she does still love me.*

Arriving at their places on the dance floor, Darcy left her on the ladies' side and strode across the way to take his place among the gentlemen. He stared at her, willing his pounding heart to slow. Finally, the first movement of the dance began. As he stepped toward her and took her hands, he had to remind himself not to pull her close. As they stepped away from each other, he took a deep breath, closing his eyes for just a moment before opening them to see Elizabeth's beautiful countenance once more.

"Have you been to Bath?" Darcy touched her hand, this time lightly, as they met in the pattern, causing her to shiver at the welcome and familiar touch.

"No, I never have," she replied with a smile.

"I thought not," Darcy replied, adding just before they parted, "I did not see you there."

Once again, the steps of the dance separated them, this time requiring that they move to other partners. When they came back together, Elizabeth had a question for Darcy.

"Were you looking, sir?" she asked.

"Always," he replied.

Now the dance required them to partner with the couple on the other side. They skipped and hopped and moved in a circle, then back into their places.

"As was I." She took his hand as they moved down the set. This was where her hand belonged—in his.

Chapter 2

When their set was over, Darcy led Elizabeth back toward the lady she had been standing with. He had discovered during their dance that the woman was Elizabeth's aunt from London, and that Elizabeth and her aunt and uncle were staying at a nearby estate.

"Did you enjoy your dance, my dear?" Maddie looked between her niece and the handsome gentleman with whom she seemed to be acquainted.

"I did, very much so." Elizabeth's smile was bright.

"Miss Bennet, would you be so kind as to introduce me to your friend?"

"Oh! Yes, I do not know why I did not before." Elizabeth blushed, but remained composed. "Mr. Darcy, this is my aunt, Mrs. Gardiner, of Gracechurch Street in London. Aunt, this is Mr. Fitzwilliam Darcy, of Pemberley in Derbyshire."

Darcy bowed. "I am pleased to meet you, madam."

Maddie curtseyed. "Likewise, sir. The two of you have met before, I think?"

"We have," Elizabeth replied.

Maddie noted the glowing smiles on the faces of the two before her.

"We met at Pemberley a few years ago." Darcy could not take his eyes off Elizabeth.

Maddie could see that both of them were enamoured of each other. She also observed that her niece had stopped searching the room the minute the gentleman had approached. "I see." She paused, not certain what, if anything, she should say next.

"May I get you a cup of punch?" Darcy asked Elizabeth, but remembered Maddie and included her. "You, as well, Mrs. Gardiner. I know that I am thirsty after such vigorous exercise and could use something to whet my throat." When both the ladies indicated that yes, they would appreciate something to drink, Darcy turned toward the refreshments table after a lingering glance at Elizabeth.

Maddie silently waited for her niece to look at her once the gentleman had walked off, silently chuckling at the besotted look on Elizabeth's face. Finally, knowing she only had a few minutes to ask, she could wait no longer. "I see that you are not searching the room anymore, Elizabeth. I also see that you are staring after Mr. Darcy and he is darting looks at you. Do you have something to tell me?"

Elizabeth sighed deeply. "Oh, Aunt. I suppose I do, but not here." Reluctantly, she pulled her eyes away from Darcy. "Do you recall earlier, when you asked me if I was still examining the people at every ball and dinner I attend?"

"I do." Maddie's full attention was on her niece.

"I *was* searching for someone, and I have found him at long last."

Maddie's brows rose almost to her hairline. "You were searching for Mr. Darcy?"

"I was."

"However did you meet him? You travel in such different circles."

"Do you remember when I and my sisters and parents went to visit Papa's sister, my Aunt Hayes?"

Now a crease appeared between Maddie's lowered brows. "I do. That was several years ago."

"It was. My aunt and uncle live in Derbyshire. They are close neighbors to the Darcys. We were often in company together." Elizabeth glanced around. Not wanting to be overheard giving details, she finished with a simple, "We became friends, Mr. Darcy and I. But then, he went on a tour and I went home, and we lost touch."

Maddie lifted her chin. "I see." She noticed Darcy working his way in their direction, holding three cups of punch up over the heads of the other guests. "It is a good thing we came tonight then, is it not?" She smiled at Elizabeth, who grinned back.

"Here we go," Darcy lowered the cups and allowed each lady to take one. Lifting his own to his mouth, he observed, "It is quite a crush here tonight. Any hostess in London would be proud to have this many guests."

"It is a good thing you are so tall, Mr. Darcy." There was a twinkle in Elizabeth's eye as she flirted with him.

"Indeed it is, Miss Bennet." Seeing their host heading their way with another gentleman, Darcy asked Elizabeth for another set of dances. "Perhaps the supper set?"

"You may certainly have those dances, sir. I will happily save them for you."

Mr. Brodie arrived just then. "It is good of you to come, Mrs. Gardiner," he exclaimed. "I just saw your husband come out of the library; he should be arriving in the ballroom soon."

Maddie laughed. "Thank you, Mr. Brodie. Mr. Gardiner finds it difficult to leave off business, even for a night. I believe he told me he was speaking to an investor."

Brodie grinned in response. "I believe you are right." Turning to Darcy, he teased, "I see that you took my advice and made yourself agreeable. You are a fine dancer. You should not hide that skill."

Darcy blushed and looked down, but a small smile lifted the corners of his mouth. "Thank you, sir." He looked up. "I found an exceptional partner."

"I saw that!" Brodie turned to Elizabeth. "Miss Bennet, you are the picture of gracefulness on the dance floor."

Elizabeth shook her head but smiled. "I thank you. A well-trained partner makes all the difference, I think." She darted a glance at Darcy, to see him staring at her.

"Speaking of partners," Brodie pulled on the arm of the young man at his side, "this gentleman has asked for an introduction. Miss Elizabeth Bennet, this is Mr. Douglas Butler. He is the heir to an estate on the other side of the county."

Elizabeth tensed, but curtseyed politely as the young redhead bowed. Pasting a smile on her face, she listened as he spoke to her with the thick Scottish brogue so common to the people of the area.

"I am pleased to meet ye." Mr. Butler seemed nervous, and Elizabeth's compassionate heart felt bad for him, but she knew what was coming and kept darting anguished looks at Darcy.

"And I, you."

Once Brodie had completed the introductions, Mr. Butler turned back to Elizabeth. "May I have this dance, Miss Bennet?"

Reluctantly, Elizabeth consented. She threw one more look in Darcy's direction, this one full of apology, and accepted the young man's arm, allowing him to lead her toward the newly forming line of dancers.

Darcy stood rigidly watching them walk away. He heard Brodie say something and then leave, but the words did not penetrate his consciousness. Jealousy roared through him at the thought of someone else touching his Elizabeth. He was brought back to his surroundings by a hand on his arm. He looked down at Mrs. Gardiner.

"I do not know you, sir, but I can see that you and my niece share an affinity for each other." Maddie waited for Darcy to nod his acknowledgement of the truth of her words. "You are aware that she must dance with others. The other guests would talk if she did not, and she would not be allowed to dance the supper set with you if she refused other gentlemen." Maddie paused, and when she saw Darcy's shoulders slump a little, continued, "My niece did not wish to give me details about your relationship here, and I will not ask you to, either. I should, however, like for you to call on us tomorrow." Maddie could see her spouse making his way towards them. "My husband and I have guardianship of Elizabeth while she is with us, and we take that responsibility very seriously."

Darcy nodded again. He had intended to ask Elizabeth for permission to call, and still would, but with Mrs. Gardiner having given her invitation, he could relax.

"Are you flirting with the younger gentlemen now, my love?" Edward Gardiner approached his wife with a tease.

Maddie laughed. "Indeed not; however, I have made a new acquaintance, who has met Elizabeth before."

Gardiner tilted his head and looked at Darcy out of the corner of his eye. "Have you now?"

"I have." Maddie grinned and turned her attention to Darcy.

Darcy cleared his throat. He was nervous and hoped to make as good an impression on Elizabeth's uncle as he seemed to have made on her aunt. "Would you introduce me?"

"Of course," Maddie smiled. "This is my husband, Mr. Edward Gardiner. Edward, this is Mr. Fitzwilliam Darcy, of Derbyshire."

"Darcy?" Gardiner's brows rose at the name, and he looked pointedly at his wife. Then, he turned his full attention to his newest acquaintance and bowed. "I am pleased to meet you, sir."

Darcy bowed in return. "And I, you. Miss Bennet has always had good things to say about you. She values you highly, both of you."

A slow smile spread over Gardiner's face. "We feel the same about her. She is a very special young woman."

"She is," Darcy agreed, his gaze wandering out to the dance floor, where Elizabeth was moving in a circle around Mr. Butler.

Gardiner took advantage of the younger man's inattention to look at Maddie once more, lifting his brows and tipping his head toward Darcy. He lifted his chin when his wife mouthed "old friends" in answer to his silent question.

Just then, Darcy looked down and turned so that he once more faced the older couple. "Mrs. Gardiner has granted me permission to call tomorrow."

"If my wife has asked you, I am eager to have you. Did she tell you where we are staying?"

"No, but Miss Bennet did. You are at Briarscraig, on the far side of Kirtlebridge?"

"We are. Mr. Reid is looking at investing in a venture, and I am here to present him the details of it."

Darcy inclined his head. "Investments are the way of the future. My father and his generation were devoted to the land, and insisted it would always take care of us, but I fear that is not so. Since he passed, I have grown Pemberley's profits greatly with careful investment of them."

Gardiner nodded. "You are correct; investment is the smart thing in these times. As you noted, it is difficult to get agreement to that out of some gentlemen. Thankfully, Mr.

Reid is not one of them." He grinned, noting Darcy's similar reaction. "Ah, the music has stopped."

Darcy had also noted the cessation of the musicians and had spun around to watch Elizabeth return on the arm of her partner.

"Thank you, Mr. Butler. I had a wonderful time." Curtseying, Elizabeth watched him bow, then turn and walk away, toward another young lady further down the room. Then, she turned to Darcy and her relatives. She let out a big sigh, then smiled brightly and said, "I see that Uncle and Mr. Darcy have been introduced."

Gardiner chuckled. "We have. We were enjoying a very diverting discussion before you wandered our direction."

"Oh, well, do not let my presence stop you." Elizabeth's eyes grew wide as she spoke. "I would not wish to distract anyone." She winked at her uncle, whose laughter grew louder.

Darcy was, as always, fascinated by Elizabeth's expressions. When she teased her uncle, Darcy's slight smile had turned into a grin as he joined her uncle in laughter. He enjoyed simply being beside her, being part of her circle. It had always been that way.

Before the next set began, another gentleman was brought over and introduced to Elizabeth. Darcy was unhappy about it, but he was even more displeased when a young

27

lady was thrust under his nose. There was no way for him to refuse to ask her to dance, and so he spent a miserable half-hour or so listening to the nattering of a lady who was not his Elizabeth.

Down the row of dancers, several places away, Elizabeth had spotted Darcy and the young woman taking their positions. Elizabeth remembered the somber look on Darcy's face. It was one he unconsciously donned when he was uncomfortable. She could well imagine the thoughts whirling around in his mind. At least, she could if his feelings for her were the same as they had been four years ago. She shared those emotions; she was jealous of the stranger for dancing with *her* Fitzwilliam and both sympathetic to his plight and upset that he danced with anyone else. For the entire set, Elizabeth's partner struggled to gain her attention. It was pointless, however, for her focus was on Darcy. She could not find it within herself to feel guilty for her actions.

Darcy's partner was equally frustrated. She used every ploy she could think of to engage the tall, handsome gentleman in conversation, but he was resistant. Not only that, his face was always turned down the line. She could swear he was watching another woman.

To the relief of both couples, the pair of dances was soon over and they could separate. Darcy and Elizabeth joined the Gardiners once more on the side of the room. The four conversed easily, with the younger falling into their previous habit of staring at each other. They were interrupted by another set of dances, and then, "The next set is the supper set, I believe."

"You are correct, Mr. Darcy!" Gardiner held out his elbow to his wife. "Come, let us eat. All this milling about and dancing has made me quite hungry."

Darcy offered his arm to Elizabeth, feeling the zing to his heart from the spot where her gloved hand rested in the crook of his elbow. As he escorted her to the dining room behind her aunt and uncle, he was proud to have her on his arm once more.

Chapter 3

The next day, heart racing in anticipation, Darcy presented himself at Briarscraig as early as was socially acceptable for a call. He followed the butler into a drawing room at the front of the house, where he found the entire household awaiting him.

"Good morning, Mr. Darcy," Gerald Reid greeted him. "How are you this fine morning?"

"I am well, sir. Yourself?"

"Never better! Have you met my wife?" Reid gestured to a petite, auburn-haired beauty standing beside him. "This is my Meg," he announced proudly.

Darcy bowed. "I am pleased to make your acquaintance."

Mrs. Reid curtseyed and then wrapped her husband's arm with her hands. "And I, you. I remember your mother visiting when you were a boy. What a handsome gentleman you have grown into. You must be a comfort to her. Did she come with you?"

"No, madam, she is in London at present."

"Well, when you write to her, please give her my regards. I hope that she makes it up our way again soon."

"I will tell her; I thank you."

Mr. Reid, hearing that the formalities had been performed between his wife and neighbour and seeing the looks Darcy was shooting in the direction of his visitors, spoke again. "I understand that you are acquainted with my guests." He stepped back, guiding his wife with him, to open a path between Darcy and the Gardiners and their niece.

"I am." Darcy caught sight of Elizabeth, and his heart stopped for a moment. She was stunning, in his eyes, in a gown of pale blue with lilac flowers embroidered along the hem and sleeves. Her hair was up, as expected, but bits of it had been curled and left to dangle out of her coiffure. Darcy could feel a grin begin to split his face as the blood began flowing through his veins once more. He bowed to her and her relatives and greeted them.

"Good morning, Mr. Darcy." Elizabeth's response had been quiet, but the glow in her eyes and the soft expression on her face let her companions know how she felt about the gentleman.

Darcy bowed over her hand, bringing it to his lips but stopping short of kissing it. He greeted the Gardiners then, but his eyes kept returning to Elizabeth.

"We will leave you to your visit, I think." Reid bowed to the group as his wife curtseyed. "Meg has called for tea to be sent up. Please, make yourself at home." Nodding to Gardiner, the gentleman and his wife turned toward the door, quietly pulling it closed behind them.

"Do sit, Mr. Darcy," Maddie waved him to the sofa where Elizabeth stood. "We are happy to see you. Elizabeth has been pacing the floors since daybreak." She winked at her blushing niece. "You would have thought the Prince Regent was coming to visit." She laughed aloud when Elizabeth rolled her eyes.

As usual, Darcy could barely keep his eyes off Elizabeth, but he had caught the wink and eyeroll that were exchanged. *I see now where my Elizabeth gets her lively and sportive manner.* He smirked and shook his head when Maddie laughed.

"I am pleased to hear that Miss Bennet thinks so highly of me as to worry about my arrival." Darcy turned back to Elizabeth and held her gaze with his eyes.

"I am likewise pleased that you did, indeed, come." Elizabeth suddenly looked down, as though fearful she had spoken out of turn.

"Were you afraid I would not?" Darcy's demeanour instantly changed as he discerned her fear.

Breathing in, Elizabeth looked up at him once more. "The last time we parted, you did not. You disappeared and I spent four years looking for you, as far as I was able."

Darcy nodded, clasping his hands together in his lap so he would not reach out and drag her to his chest and hold her. With her guardians in the room, he needed to carefully observe propriety. Not that he would

33

Zoe Burton

treat her cavalierly in any case. He would not, but had they been alone, he would have been more comfortable demonstrating his continued affection and care in a physical manner. "I am sorry for that. My mother insisted I leave immediately. I did not have opportunity to even inform my valet that he needed to pack my things."

"Yes; your father told me that your mother demanded you be sent away at once. He apologized to me for it."

"My father liked you very much. He did not share my mother's feelings on the subject of my future marriage."

Elizabeth smiled. "I liked him, as well." She put her hand on Darcy's arm. "I was sorry to hear of his passing a few years ago. Aunt Hayes wrote me of it."

"Thank you. It was difficult. It still is, to be honest, but the pain has receded to more of a dull ache." Darcy blinked away the tears that seemed to always torment him when he thought of the elder Darcy. Elizabeth held out her handkerchief to him, and he thanked her with a smile as he blotted his eyes. Then, in full view of her aunt and uncle, Darcy kissed the handkerchief and tucked it into his pocket.

"Elizabeth has shared with us some of what happened that summer, sir." Gardiner watched the couple carefully. "I cannot help but feel that she has not shared the entire story."

Darcy and Elizabeth both blushed. "I do not know what she has told you, but with her permission, I will tell you all." He looked at Elizabeth, his eyes questioning, and when she nodded, he began to speak, telling the Gardiners the entire tale of their romance.

"I knew I would ask Elizabeth to marry me, but my mother browbeat my father into obedience to her wishes before I could do so." Darcy had, over the course of his retelling, laid his hand over hers on his arm. "I have looked for Elizabeth everywhere I went, especially in London. I knew she had relatives there, and there was always hope that our paths would cross at the museum or the theatre.

"When I came home from my tour, I discovered that the friendship between my mother and the Hayes family had diminished. They no longer spent the time together that they had in the past, and my mother could not seem to find anything good to say about them." Darcy looked apologetically at Elizabeth. "I heard a rumor from another neighbour that you and your family were also sent away at that time; that my mother had gone to Rocky Hills and carried on so much about wanting you gone that your father felt he had to take you all home so his sister would have peace. Your aunt and uncle were so offended that they never again visited Pemberley."

Elizabeth nodded. "That is true. Your father came along on the first visit Lady Anne made. That is when he told me that he had not wanted to send you away. Aunt Hayes was furious. Every time she writes, she apologizes again."

Darcy nodded, glancing at the Gardiners. "May we have a few moments of privacy?" he asked. "Perhaps we could move to the other end of the room." He tipped his head toward the place he mentioned.

"Certainly," Gardiner agreed. "We can still see you from where we sit, and I would imagine you have things to say to each other that you would not wish others to hear."

Darcy rose, bringing Elizabeth with him. "Thank you, sir."

In less than a minute, the couple was settled on a couch several feet away, and they continued their conversation.

"I did not wish to go." Darcy's voice was soft, her hand held tightly in his.

Elizabeth lifted her free hand to caress his cheek. "I know. It was not your fault; you would never have left me on your own."

Darcy's eyes closed at her touch and he smiled gently. Opening them again, he asked, "Can you forgive me?"

"Sir, there is nothing to forgive. It was not your fault." With a final stroke, Elizabeth dropped her hand from his face. She looked deep into his eyes. "It was the fault of Lady Anne, and to a lesser extent, your father. You had nothing to do with it. It was your duty to honour your parents and you did. I am proud of you for that." She paused. "That sense of duty is part of the reason I love you as I do."

"Still, after all this time?" Darcy felt joy rising inside.

Elizabeth's lips widened into a smile. "Yes, even now. My heart has not wavered, not in four years. Has yours?"

"You know it has not. My heart is now as it ever was: yours." Darcy saw the delight in Elizabeth's mien and wished with all his heart to kiss her, but just as he leaned forward to do so, Gardiner cleared his throat. Darcy forced himself to sit back, but could not wipe the grin from his face. And he refused to release her hand. "Perhaps we should return and share our news with your aunt and uncle."

"Yes, we should," Elizabeth replied with a matching grin.

Elizabeth's relatives were just as happy as she was with her news.

"I feel that I must inquire, does your mother still live?" Maddie's brows were creased in concern.

"She does, and before you ask, no, she has not changed her opinion. She has spent four years throwing heiresses into my path."

"Is she aware that you still carry a *tendre* for Elizabeth?" Gardiner's expression matched that of his wife.

"She should be, given that I have resisted her every effort for four long years, but we have only spoken once about Elizabeth, and that was right after I came home following my father's death." Darcy spoke matter-of-factly. "Our relationship has been strained by her actions that summer and by her continued insistence on choosing my wife." He paused as anger suddenly began to take hold of him. "Forgive me; whenever I think about this subject, I become infuriated all over again."

Gardiner had another question. "Are you certain you wish to resume your relationship with Elizabeth, knowing that your mother does not favour her? You surely knew the name of her father's estate, and yet, you did not search for her."

"Oh, yes," Darcy replied. His hand tightened on Elizabeth's as he looked her uncle in the eye. "Quite certain. I am my own man, master of my estate. My mother may have orchestrated my father's life, but she will not control mine." He paused to breathe deeply, and then continued. "I was so busy with the aftermath of my father's death, going through the court system and learning to manage the estate on my own, that I had little time to do ought else. What time I did have, my mother took up. She needed this or that, or wished me to take her here or there, or meet this young woman or that. I was frankly exhausted. I did not have the strength to fight her, between my grief and her demands. I wished more than anything to ride to Hertfordshire and find you," he added, looking at Elizabeth, "but was unable."

Though Elizabeth was relieved to hear Darcy's declaration, she needed assurances that he would not come to regret a connection to her. "I do not wish to come between you and your mother." She examined his face, carefully searching for his true opinion. "I would not want you to begin to detest me in a few years."

Darcy squeezed Elizabeth's hand. "I promise you, Elizabeth: now that I have found you, nothing but you can separate us. Even then, if you should suddenly decide we do not suit, I will chase you down and persuade you that you are wrong." He held his breath, waiting for her next words. *What will I do if she rejects me? I cannot live without her.* His fears were relieved when she made her reply.

Elizabeth laid her free hand over Darcy's where it clasped hers. "Thank you. I feel the same."

"Good, good," Gardiner released a breath he had been holding. Then, he clasped his arms on the chair and rose, saying, "Why do we not all take a turn about the garden? After such an excess of emotion, I could use some fresh air."

His companions consented, and the four of them withdrew through the glass doors out into the well-tended flower beds and paths. They explored at first as a group. After a while, the Gardiners sat on a pretty marble bench under a tree while Darcy and Elizabeth continued on.

"Mr. Reid has a maze here," Elizabeth noted, a wave of her hand indicating the opening in a row of hedges that marked the entrance to the complexly laid out shrubbery. "I did not find it altogether challenging, though he did say that others have gotten lost in it and had to call for help getting out."

Without a word, Darcy steered Elizabeth in the direction of the hedge. Once inside, he gave her leave to lead him through the maze, saying, "I do not mind getting lost, either."

Elizabeth laughed at his wink and proceeded to escort him to the centre. They talked as they wandered their way along the paths and turnings, giving each other an overview of their time apart.

When they got to the center, they stopped and turned to face each other. Darcy took Elizabeth's hands in his, holding them tightly and gazing at her beloved face. "I feared I would never see you again," he whispered. "I looked everywhere, searched every face. I would see a girl with dark hair and examine her closely, hope rising within me, only to be disappointed when she turned and was not you." He lifted one hand and bestowed a gentle kiss on the back. "I will not lose you again." He dropped to one knee, still retaining his grasp on her hands. "Elizabeth Bennet, I love you. I always have and I always will. Tell me you will stay with me forever. Tell me you will marry me."

Tears welled up in Elizabeth's eyes as she listened to Darcy's impassioned plea. "Yes," she replied. "I have loved you since the first time I saw you, and I will happily marry you."

Darcy's joy at Elizabeth's answer could not be contained. He grinned, jumping up and pulling her into his arms. "You have made me the happiest of men," he said as his eyes roved her face. "I love you." With those words, he lowered his head and tasted her lips.

Chapter 4

When they could no longer go without taking a breath, Darcy and Elizabeth tore their lips apart, breathing heavily. "I love you." They spoke at the same time, then dissolved into laughter. Behind them was a marble bench similar to the one the Gardiners sat on outside, and Darcy pulled Elizabeth over to it, sitting down and then pulling her onto his lap.

"When can we marry?"

Elizabeth tilted her head and looked at him. "I confess; I should like to do it as soon as possible."

"I would, as well." Darcy's brow furrowed as he contemplated their options.

"Will your mother be a problem?" Elizabeth wiggled a bit in his lap to find a more comfortable position.

"She will surely try to be," Darcy declared. As he spoke, he thought about Lady Anne.

"How will she react, do you think?"

Darcy's eyebrows rose as he made a face and shrugged. "It is difficult to say for certain, but I know it will not be good. I did not tell your aunt and uncle this, and I will if I must, but my mother is manipulative as well as controlling. I do not allow her to tell me what I will and will not do, but she can be vicious when crossed. More than once, she has kept me from seeing my sister when she did not like my decisions."

"Oh, poor Georgiana! If she is as sweet as she was when I knew her, she must be heartbroken at it." Elizabeth stopped playing with the hair at Darcy's collar, her focus now wholly on his voice.

"She is. She does not understand our mother's ways. Georgiana was far closer to Papa than to Mama, and he protected her from my mother's wrath as much as he could. When he died, Georgiana was devastated and fearful. There is little I can do about it. Father left guardianship to Mother." Darcy lapsed into silence for a few minutes. He ran his hand up and down Elizabeth's arm as he continued to think.

Elizabeth elected to remain silent, sensing that Darcy had more to say. Finally, her patience was rewarded.

"I would like to try to sway my mother to my side, so that she does not abscond with my sister when I marry you." Darcy looked Elizabeth in the eye again. "Because I *will* marry you. I was serious about tracking you down." Elizabeth's smile sparked a similar one on Darcy's face, and he continued, "I do not wish to wait, though. I have a proposal, but it may not be one you like. Will you hear me out before you say anything?"

Thoughtfully, Elizabeth examined Darcy's expression. It was clear to her that he was serious and perhaps even nervous about what he wanted to tell her. "I will."

Taking a deep breath, Darcy began. "I propose that we elope, and that we keep the marriage secret for a little while. My mother has friends everywhere, and I am quite certain someone at last night's ball is even now composing a letter to her, telling her how I danced twice with a young lady. I expect a summons, at the least, ordering me home. I will ignore it, of course, but I expect it to come nonetheless. At some point in the future, we can make an announcement and take up our lives as husband and wife. What do you say?"

Elizabeth took a deep breath and let it out on a sigh. "I do not know. Part of me eagerly wishes to do it, but another part wonders if the situation is all that drastic. What is it you fear? That she will keep Georgiana from you?"

"In part, yes." Darcy fell silent for a moment. "I want to know that, no matter what, we are tied to each other, bound together forever. No one can force you to marry someone else because I'm not there, and no one can trap me into marriage, either."

Elizabeth considered Darcy's response. "We seem to always be in agreement," she finally said, smiling tenderly at him. "I also

45

want to know that we can never be torn away from each other."

"What do you think of my idea, then?"

"To be married but separated breaks my heart, but as long as I know we will be together sooner rather than later, I can bear it." Elizabeth lifted her head and pushed slightly away from Darcy. "I want your word that any separation will not be a long one. No more than a few weeks."

"I promise you it will not be long; a month or two at most." Darcy used one hand to tuck a loose tendril of hair behind Elizabeth's ear. "I do not think we should tell the Gardiners, either. I cannot explain it, but I have a feeling deep inside that they should remain unaware."

"If they do not know, then they cannot tell your mother anything." Elizabeth agreed to keep it to herself. "When shall we marry, then? And, where?"

"We are only a few miles from Gretna Green. Do you object to marrying there? It need not be in a blacksmith shop. We can marry in a church."

Elizabeth nodded. "That would be wonderful, but why not the church here?"

"If we wish to keep it a secret, we need to go to Gretna. The rector of the church here is a gossip; he would not be able to keep the marriage to himself."

"Then Gretna Green it is. The only question that remains is when."

Darcy lifted her hand to kiss it. "It will take me a few days to arrange things. What do you say to a week from today?"

Elizabeth grinned. "I say that sounds wonderful." She leaned her head down to kiss him.

Bonnyvale Estate, the same day

Elspeth Brodie sat at her writing desk to compose a letter. In truth, it was Lady Anne Darcy's turn to send her one, but Elspeth was too delighted with young Mr. Darcy to wait to share her news.

Elspeth and Lady Anne had become friends more than two decades ago, on Lady Anne's first visit to the Darcy estate in Scotland. They had kept up a regular correspondence ever since, though the letters had begun coming further apart once the two ladies began having children. Elspeth was certain her friend would be proud of the way her son had danced last night, and that his behaviour was so proper, unlike many young men his age.

Bonnyvale, Scotland

My dearest Lady Anne,

Though you have yet to reply to my last missive, I have news that I simply cannot keep to myself. I was aston-

47

ished to see your son, Fitzwilliam, at my ball last night! You sly thing, not telling me he was coming to the area. If I did not think so well of you, I might be offended.

Anyway, Fitzwilliam is all grown up now, and I was shocked to see it. The last time I saw him, he was still a gangly youth on a fishing trip with his father, during a school vacation. I always knew he would be a handsome man, and he is! And his behaviour last night! It was everything right and good, and he danced with at least two of the girls in attendance. No leaving ladies along the wall for him!

I know how highly you must think of young Fitzwilliam, and that is as it should be. He has turned out very well.

In other news, the ball, which I told you in my last letter was meant to celebrate my dear Michael's birthday, was a smashing success! A crush, as you in England would say. Our house was filled with people, all wishing my darling husband a happy day.

Mrs. Reid and her husband are hosting a couple from London and their niece. They are a friendly pair, and the niece is attractive. I saw Fitzwilliam speaking to them for a long while, and *dancing with the girl. Forgive me; I have quite forgotten their names. Now that I think of it, Fitzwilliam danced with the young lady twice. Interesting.*

I hear my youngest coming down the hall. Aiden is forever finding creatures to bring into the house. I hope he has not done so today.

I look forward to your next letter, my dear friend. Though, now you owe me two.

Yours, as ever,

Elspeth Brodie

Darcy House, London, a week later

"The mail, Madam."

The butler held out a silver salver holding just one missive. Lady Anne Darcy lifted the letter and examined it. Recognizing the handwriting, she dismissed the servant and broke open the seal. She began to read, leisurely at first, then more rapidly. She gasped, turning red, and then returned to the top of the page and read once more. Crinkling the missive in her hands, she jumped up to vigourously ring the bell, then rushed to the door. It opened before she could touch the handle.

"At your service, Madam." Mr. Baxter bowed.

"Call for my travelling coach at once. I am leaving for Glenmoor House immediately."

Baxter blinked, his astonishment clear. "Scotland, Madam?"

"Yes, Scotland," Lady Anne snapped. "After you order the coach readied, send a groom to me. I will have a letter for him to take to Henley Place."

Baxter was certain the master would not wish his mother to travel after dark, and Scotland was days away. Though he knew very well that it would anger Lady Anne, it was his duty to try to persuade her to wait until the next morning to leave. "If I may be so bold, Madam, Scotland is far away, and the trip takes days. You might be better served to allow your maid time to pack everything you will need for your comfort as you travel. If you depart immediately, she will not have time to properly prepare."

Lady Anne stared at the retainer. Though she was not of a mind to be gainsaid, she could see the sense in his words. Her lips compressed in a thin line and her jaw clenched as she attempted to rein in her anger at the delay. "Very well. You are correct, I suppose. I still wish for someone to deliver a letter immediately, but you may tell the coachman that we will leave early tomorrow. And inform Ruth that she is to begin packing right now. I will not be delayed in the morning while she finishes."

Baxter bowed, murmuring, "Yes, Madam," as Lady Anne brushed past him and hurried up the stairs.

The next morning, Lady Anne boarded her travelling coach, ordering the coachman to drive around the corner to the home of her friend, Lady Barbara Henley. Once there, she disembarked, scurrying into the house and coming out again a few minutes later with another woman in tow. They ascended into the equipage and it began to move.

Inside, Lady Anne looked across at her friend's daughter and smiled. "Trust me, Lady Clarice, my son will not be able to resist your charms. We will have you married within a year."

A smirk spread across Lady Clarice's lips. "Thank you. I look forward to it."

Chapter 5

It took Darcy five days to get the wedding arranged. His biggest concern was choosing a location at which to meet Elizabeth and take her to Gretna. He and Elizabeth talked about it several times, but could not reach an agreement.

"There is no reason I cannot meet you out by the road, Fitzwilliam," Elizabeth insisted as they strolled the gardens at Briarscraig. "I do not understand why you object so strenuously. I have been walking alone for far further distances since I was eight years old. It is barely a mile! I walked further than that to meet you in Derbyshire."

"You did. However, you were far more familiar with the area, both around Longbourn and between your aunt's estate and mine. You have only been in Scotland a few weeks, and have only left Briarscraig three or four times. It is not safe to walk in the dark in a place you do not know well." Darcy was insistent. Looking at Elizabeth, he could see that he had not convinced her, so he decided to play on her heartstrings. Stopping her, he turned her toward him, placing his hands on her shoulders. "If anything were to happen to you, if you were injured or killed, I would not be able to live with myself. The guilt and grief would eat at me until I could not handle any more." Darcy watched the firmness of her jaw soften and her eyes fill with tears, and knew he had finally changed her mind.

"Very well. I will do as you wish and allow you to meet me at the servant's door." Elizabeth, mindful of her aunt's chaperonage, squeezed Darcy's arm instead of caressing his cheek as she wished to.

In the end, the point became moot when the Reids decided to host a ball in their home. Darcy would be able to spend the night, as would several other guests whose estates were further away. He could collect Elizabeth from her room instead of on the grounds or at the side of the road.

During the time that Darcy was making plans, he visited Elizabeth nearly every day. The Gardiners and Reids left them alone several times, and he knew they were wondering why there was no announcement made.

"My aunt and uncle look at me strangely every now and again," Elizabeth told him on one of those occasions. "I say nothing to them, but I cannot help but wonder why they do not ask."

"Yes, your uncle has begun looking askance at me when we gentlemen are apart from you ladies. Maybe he and your aunt have decided that since you do not seem unhappy, they will not get involved."

"That could be," Elizabeth replied, tilting her head and looking past Darcy as she considered the situation. Turning her face back to his, she added, "Aunt Maddie has hinted strongly that they expect at least a courtship out of us. I do fear they will worry when we leave in a little over a fortnight and nothing has been said."

"Do you think we should take them into our confidence, at least with a few of the facts?"

Elizabeth blinked, surprised that he had inquired after their decision to keep their marriage a secret. "I suppose we could. I trust them completely. They will not gossip, even to tell the Reids, if we ask them to keep it to themselves. How much do you want to say to them?"

"I think it would ease their mind to know that we are courting—which we are, that is not a lie—and keeping quiet about it because of Georgiana, and that when we have convinced my mother to accept you, we will announce it publicly. What do you think?"

Elizabeth pursed her lips and gave the idea some thought. Coming to a decision, she assured him that she agreed. "I think that is an excellent idea. When do you wish to have this discussion?"

"Before I leave today, I think."

The Gardiners were very understanding, having suspected as much when the young couple remained silent on the subject but Darcy was in almost-constant attendance on Elizabeth.

"You certainly have my permission to court Elizabeth," Gardiner exclaimed when Darcy asked him.

"We will not tell a soul," Maddie assured Darcy. "I am simply happy that Elizabeth has found you again. It is clear that you are deeply in love; I am certain that, once your mother sees it, she will not be able to keep from loving my niece as much as you do."

Though Darcy heartily doubted it was possible, he only thanked Maddie for her kind words and understanding.

Darcy kept Elizabeth apprised of his progress in planning their elopement. Every time he visited, they walked the gardens, often disappearing into the maze for five or ten minutes of conversation and kisses. Finally, the day before the ball, Darcy arrived with his valet, having been invited to do so by the Reids. He and Elizabeth chose on this day to wander the rose gardens, within sight of her aunt but far enough away that Maddie could not hear their conversation.

"All is prepared, Elizabeth. Shall we away tonight?"

Elizabeth turned a beaming smile up at Darcy, both hands wrapped around his arm. She squeezed his limb close to her side. "Yes. I can hardly believe the time has come. I am eager to be your wife."

Darcy grinned at her enthusiasm. He brought his free hand up to rest it on hers. "I am eager to be your husband," he replied. "I will collect you from your room after the house settles for the night. I hope you do not mind if we ride, instead of taking a carriage. Riding will get us there faster. Have you a cloak with a hood?"

"I do," Elizabeth assured him. "I will be ready."

Later that night, after the household retired, Elizabeth allowed her maid to help her prepare for bed. Then, when the girl had been dismissed, she got back up and dressed herself once more, this time in a riding habit and her half-boots. Swirling her cape around her and tying it on, she paced the room, avoiding the spot where the floorboards creaked. Finally, after what seemed like hours but could not have been more than a few minutes, she heard a soft knock. Rushing to the door, she opened it and saw Darcy standing in the weak light of a candle. Taking his hand with one of hers and using the other to pull her hood up over her head, she allowed him to lead her down the hallway to the servant's stairs and out to the stable. There, she waited as he saddled a large horse. Soon, they were both mounted on the great beast's back and riding slowly away from Briarscraig.

Once out on the road and away from the house and stable, Darcy urged the gelding into a trot and then a canter. Even with alternating the horse's gait, he and Elizabeth arrived in Gretna Green an hour after starting out. He pulled them to a stop in front of a church. Seeing a light glowing from the window, he nodded in satisfaction and then dismounted. He reached up and assisted Elizabeth, holding her waist and allowing her to slide down against him with her hands on his shoulders. When she was on her feet on the ground, he bent his head to hers and kissed her. "Are you ready for this?"

"I am." Elizabeth stood on her tiptoes to kiss Darcy again, and then accepted the arm he held out.

As Darcy led her toward the church door, Elizabeth all at once felt a flurry of butterflies inside. She pressed her free hand to her stomach to calm them, but the fluttering did not stop. Her palms began to sweat beneath her gloves. Biting her lip, she glanced up at Darcy just as he looked down at her. Seeing the love in his expression—the softness of his features, the directness of his gaze as he looked into her eyes, and the small smile that lifted the corners of his lips—her nerves immediately settled. She smiled back at him, then turned her head forward and squared her shoulders. She was marrying the love of her life and was eager to bind herself to him forever. She stepped through the doorway and into the darkened lobby. At Darcy's urging, she moved into the dimly lit sanctuary, where a priest, another man, and a woman waited in front of the altar.

In a few short seconds, Elizabeth stood beside her beloved, reciting wedding vows. The ceremony was brief, given the early morning hour and the lack of audience. They signed the register and mounted the gelding once more, headed back to Briarscraig. As they rode, they talked.

"How were you able to persuade the rector to marry us at such an hour?" Elizabeth had been amazed at the man's willingness— cheerfulness, even—to forgo sleep to perform the duty. She felt the shrug of Darcy's shoulders behind her.

"One of the first things I learned when I took over Pemberley was that money will buy me almost anything I could ever want. I offered the man a large donation in exchange for his services."

Elizabeth's brows rose. "How much did you give him?"

"Probably enough to operate the church for a full year, including his salary and alms for the needy."

"Really?" Elizabeth had long known the Darcys were wealthy, but she had never before considered what that really meant. She settled her back against her new husband's chest and considered this. Finally, she said, "I am simply happy that he was willing to perform the ceremony, despite the expense."

Darcy kissed her hair. "You are worth every penny, my love."

Elizabeth tilted her head back and up to see his face. "Thank you. I love you."

Darcy kissed her lips, then, briefly. "I love you."

They arrived back at the Reids' estate and quietly approached the stables. After unsaddling the horse, they snuck back into the house the way they had left. Darcy entered Elizabeth's room, not leaving until just before the servants began to stir.

An hour or so later, both appeared in the dining room to break their fasts, albeit separately. Elizabeth entered the room first, finding it empty. She knew she was a little early, but despite the lack of sleep from her long night of activity, she was wide awake. Since the sideboard was already filled with tempting goodies, she made herself a plate and sat at the table. A footman poured her a cup of tea, and she thanked him. She was still nibbling on a sweet roll when the Gardiners entered the room.

"Good morning, Lizzy," Maddie greeted her niece before filling her own plate. "How did you sleep?"

Smiling to herself, Elizabeth replied, "I had a wonderful night, Aunt."

"Excellent." Maddie looked at her husband, who was not his best before his first cup or two of coffee. "Edward, shall I fix you a plate?"

Gardiner waved his hand at her and nodded, then shook out the newspaper and began reading. He snatched up his coffee cup the moment the footman had it filled.

Elizabeth giggled softly at her uncle. She had always found it amusing how he needed his favorite beverage before he could speak to anyone in the mornings.

The three were soon joined by their hosts, and then Darcy. His eyes locked onto Elizabeth's the moment he saw her, and she returned the look. Though the others in the room were aware of the attraction—and the Gardiners knew why there was no courtship announcement—none of them knew just how deep that attachment was, and that knowledge fanned the flames of passion that Darcy and Elizabeth shared. Blushing suddenly, they looked away from each other.

After Darcy had selected some ham and toast from the sideboard, he returned to the table and sat beside Elizabeth. They spoke together quietly as they ate.

Chapter 6

Darcy and Elizabeth were inseparable the entire day. After the delights they had discovered upon their return from Gretna Green, they were anxious to be alone once more but found it difficult to do so with the Reids and Gardiners all acting as chaperones.

"I know it was my suggestion to keep our marriage a secret, and that we have good reason to do so, but I begin to regret it. We have not been alone long enough today to do more than steal a kiss," Darcy complained, his mouth hovering over the side of Elizabeth's neck, where he was planting lingering kisses.

Elizabeth tilted her head to give Darcy better access. She smirked at his words but heartily agreed. "Yes, I believe we should have given it all a bit more thought. If not for this puzzle of greenery, we would not even be able to steal the kisses we have. Are you certain you wish to continue with the ruse?"

Darcy stopped his distracting activity to look Elizabeth straight in the eye. "As much as I abhor deception of every kind, it is important to our continued happiness to do so. It will only be a few weeks, as I have already promised you. I will make my mother see reason, and then we will begin our lives together openly."

Elizabeth stroked his cheek. "Very well, then, Mr. Darcy. We shall continue with our plan." She turned her head as she heard her aunt's voice calling her name. Looking at Darcy again, she said, "Kiss me quickly, Husband. I am being summoned."

Darcy complied and then led Elizabeth out of the shrubbery and toward her aunt.

"There you are! I told your uncle that you were well by yourselves, but he insisted I come find you." Maddie winked at her niece.

Elizabeth blushed. "We had some things to discuss. I apologize if we took longer than we should have."

"It was nothing, I assure you. Your uncle can be quite the worrier at times." Maddie chuckled. "He trusts you both, he says, yet he wants to know your location at all times." She shook her head.

Elizabeth covered her mouth with her hand, smothering a giggle. "Poor Uncle," she cried, "to be teased so when he is not present to defend himself!"

Maddie rolled her eyes. "Turnabout is fair play, I believe."

The three of them entered the house through the drawing room, where the Reids had a tea service laid out.

"Did you have a pleasant walk? The gardens are so beautiful at this time of year!" Meg Reid asked Elizabeth as the younger woman settled on a settee.

"We did." Elizabeth watched as Darcy lowered himself beside her. "Mr. Darcy and I walked through the maze again. I believe he is beginning to know the paths as well as I." She winked at him when he grinned at her.

Mr. Reid laughed. "Do not share your knowledge with my other guests, please! I gain far too much enjoyment from that structure to have the secret spread about, you know."

"I will take it to my grave, I assure you." Darcy placed his hand over his heart, but his chuckle gave away his amusement.

"Miss Bennet, you have had a letter, I believe. I gave it to your aunt." Meg began to pour out the tea, handing the cups to a waiting maid to pass around.

"I almost forgot! You do have a note. I think it must be from your friend, Charlotte, for I do not recognize the handwriting." Maddie dug around in her reticule for the missive, pulling it out with a flourish and handing it to her niece.

Elizabeth took it with thanks, and said, as she examined the direction written on the front, "Yes, it is from Charlotte. I will read it later." Elizabeth placed the letter in her own reticule, and then accepted a cup of tea.

The conversation turned to other things, then, mostly the ball that evening. It was not until hours later, when Elizabeth met Darcy for a walk through the gallery, that she was able to read her letter.

"What does your friend have to say?"

Elizabeth folded the letter up and tucked it back into her reticule as she replied, "She is well. She tells me that all is in preparation for my visit next month." Elizabeth tucked her hand under Darcy's elbow. "I am suddenly dreading it, you know."

Darcy tilted his head as he looked at her, "Because of our marriage?" When Elizabeth nodded, he placed his free hand over hers and caressed her fingers. Turning his gaze to the front, he steered her around a seating area and strolled on. "I confess to feeling similarly. I did not realize when we planned this how difficult it would be to be your husband but not be able to share that fact."

"It is a struggle." Elizabeth readily agreed with him. "We have been married not even a full day, and I chafe at the restrictions. However, I do not wish for you and your sister to be denied access to each other, either."

"No," Darcy sighed. "If only my mother were not so mulish, so ... determined to have her own way. What I would not give to be able to go to my only remaining parent, the one who is supposed to be the gentler one, and tell her my good news with the expectation of joy on her part." Darcy tensed as his temperature rose. He worked to control his emotions, determined to be a gentleman at all times.

Elizabeth felt his tension rising. She squeezed his arm close to her side. "Do not allow her to rule your feelings, Fitzwilliam. I know you are angry at her for separating us. I am, as well. But, as you said to my uncle just a few days ago, you are your own man. She will either accept me as your wife and us as a couple or she will not. Either way, we will face it together. We have found each other again, and have made it so that we cannot be permanently separated ever again. She has not won, my love. We have."

Darcy stopped walking as Elizabeth made her impassioned speech. Turning toward her, he held her hands in his, caressing his thumbs over the backs of them. He took a deep breath when she finished and looked down at the floor. Then, looking up, he stared into her eyes and said, "You are so wise for someone who is not yet one and twenty. I am not certain what I have done to deserve you, but I have you, and I will never let you go. I love you, Elizabeth Darcy." His last words were spoken on a whisper, and he leaned forward to caress her lips with his. Pulling her into his arms, he deepened the kiss, and they lost themselves in the feelings of passion that always seemed to rise when they were together.

The sound of servants speaking in the next room as they prepared for the ball brought Darcy and Elizabeth back to their senses, and they separated.

"We should be preparing for the ball." Elizabeth longed to be back in Darcy's arms, but knew that would have to wait.

"Yes," Darcy sighed again. "Come, I will escort you to your chambers."

With a tender smile, Elizabeth once again accepted the arm Darcy offered, and they silently made their way up the stairs and to the guest wing. He left her standing at her door after kissing her hand. When he had opened the door to his own room, looked back at her, waved, and disappeared, she turned and entered her chamber.

~~~***~~~

A few hours later, the Reids were occupied with welcoming their guests, and the Gardiners, Elizabeth, and Darcy were in the ballroom, admiring the splendor and speaking with the early arrivals. Though Darcy and Elizabeth were, as always, within an arm's reach of each other at all times, they managed to hide the depth of their feelings. They maintained the image of being mere acquaintances for most of the night, though they were unable to stay completely away from each other.

About halfway through the evening, just after the supper set had begun, Darcy approached Elizabeth and requested that she take a turn about the garden with him. She acquiesced, and they proceeded out the door and onto the balcony. There were other couples on the lawn, parading back and forth, and the Darcys joined them. However, Darcy soon separated Elizabeth from the rest of the guests, and they snuck up the servant's stairs to his room for a private tete-a-tete. They returned to the ballroom, separately, just as the last notes of the second dance of the set faded away. The Gardiners had been dancing, as had the Reids, and the rest of the guests were involved in their own entertainments. So, no one noticed the flush that graced Elizabeth's skin or Darcy's slightly swollen lips.

~~~***~~~

For the next several days, Darcy and Elizabeth worked hard finding ways and places to be alone, and to hide their growing intimacy from everyone else in the house. Darcy had been forced to return to Glenmoor lest his continued presence raise eyebrows among the Reids and their neighbours. He continued to see Elizabeth every day, though.

The couple had been married less than a week when Darcy arrived to find Mrs. Reid and the ladies entertaining Mrs. Elspeth Brodie and her eldest daughter, Edith.

"Why, Mr. Darcy, what brings you here to Briarscraig?" Mrs. Brodie was happy to see the gentleman once more. "I was delighted to see you dance at the ball a few days ago. I remember how shy and reserved you were as a young boy."

Meg, knowing that Elspeth was a gossip, did her best to shield Darcy from an interrogation. "Mr. Darcy has visited us on several occasions. He has been excellent company."

Darcy lifted the corner of his lips in a half-smile. "Thank you, Madam. I have been discussing business with Mr. Reid and Mr. Gardiner, mostly. I have, however, greatly enjoyed the company of the ladies of the house, as well."

"Oh, that is right!" Elspeth turned to Maddie. "Your husband is here on business with Reid. I had forgotten."

"Yes," Maddie replied with a smile. "I believe my husband and the other gentlemen have concluded the actual business and are now simply enjoying each other's company."

Elspeth smiled at Maddie, but her attention was still set on Darcy, who had settled into a chair placed a little apart from the ladies. "I am surprised to see you here, to be honest. I had thought you would be preparing for your mother's arrival."

Darcy's brows rose almost to his hairline. He had not received a letter from Lady Anne since he had come to Scotland, and was not aware that she corresponded with anyone here, though he had suspected it. "My mother?"

"Why, yes! I had a note from her yesterday, sent express. She said she would arrive at Glenmoor in two days. She was somewhere in Yorkshire, as I understand it."

Darcy's heart stopped beating for a few seconds at Mrs. Brodie's words. He forced himself not to glance at his beloved, not wishing to give the visitor, who was obviously in contact with his mother, any reason to suspect something might be going on between him and Elizabeth. "I have not received a letter. I will have to ask the housekeeper when I return home if one has perhaps been misplaced." Darcy blew out a silent breath when his voice did not display the distress that he felt.

"Oh, I am sorry; I assumed you knew. I hope I did not ruin a surprise."

Darcy hurried to reassure the lady. "All is well. Lady Anne sometimes forgets to inform me of her coming and going. I suspect she still sees me as a boy more often than not." He was relieved that his small joke distracted the ladies into changing the topic of conversation.

Chapter 7

A few minutes later, Reid and Gardiner entered the room ahead of the maid with the tea service, and within a half-hour, Elspeth Brodie and her daughter were back in their carriage and heading home. Darcy immediately asked Elizabeth to walk with him in the garden.

Elizabeth had been alarmed at Mrs. Brodie's words. She had been forced to shake off the dizziness and trembling that had come upon her in order to pay attention. For the remainder of the lady's visit, Elizabeth had held herself in rigid control, a smile plastered to her face. When Darcy requested her company, she readily agreed, accepting his hand to help her rise and following him through the corridor and out the library's folding glass doors.

"Are you well, my love?" Darcy was concerned about Elizabeth. He had seen her go pale when Mrs. Brodie had mentioned his mother, and it had taken all he had to remain in place. "I wanted to come to your side, but if my mother and Mrs. Brodie are writing letters back and forth, I do not wish for her to suspect anything."

"I am well," Elizabeth assured him, though she could hear the lingering shakiness of her voice. "I was shocked to hear the news, is all."

"I was, as well," Darcy admitted. He lifted his gaze from the ground in front of his feet to look around the sky and the treetops around them. Then, after throwing a glance behind him to see if anyone was close enough to hear, he looked back at Elizabeth and asked, "What do you think, Wife? Might we be able to live together sooner than we thought?"

"I hope so," Elizabeth declared with fervency. "I fear she will not be so easily swayed, however."

"We will know soon enough, I suppose." They had approached the maze, and Darcy led Elizabeth inside, unerringly making his way to the center. There, he sat on the bench and pulled his wife into his lap. It was one of his favorite ways to hold her, and offered him a great sense of comfort. He knew Elizabeth enjoyed it, as well, and so he felt free to employ this method as often as he could get away with. The couple spent several minutes reassuring each other of their love and that all would be well before they rejoined the Gardiners and Reids.

~~~***~~~

Two days later, Darcy was preparing to leave for Briarscraig when the front door was flung open and his mother sauntered in. Immediately tensing, Darcy narrowed his eyes when Lady Anne was followed by a young lady. Once the girl looked up, Darcy groaned inside, for he recognized the woman as the daughter of one of his mother's friends and the heiress she was currently intent on throwing at his head.

"There you are, Fitzwilliam. Come into the drawing room. I would have a word with you." Lady Anne turned to the housekeeper. "Show Lady Clarice to her room."

Darcy interceded. "Mrs. MacIntire has not prepared a chamber for Lady Clarice, because I did not know she was accompanying you. Come to think of it, the only reason *you* have a room ready, Mother, is because Mrs. Brodie informed me that you were on your way." Turning to the housekeeper, he politely requested a room be readied for their unexpected guest. "Give her the rose room, Mrs. MacIntire."

Lady Anne gave a cry. "No, she should have a room in the family wing. Do not listen to him, MacIntire. I insist she be placed next to me."

"Mrs. MacIntire knows who pays her wages, Mother, and she follows my orders, not yours. The rose room, if you please." Darcy sent the housekeeper off with a jerk of his head and she quickly scurried away to do his bidding. Darcy turned back to Lady Anne. "You may await your rooms in the library. I will call for tea. I was on my way out when you arrived."

"You will attend us." Lady Anne stood rigidly, chin lifted as she looked down her nose at her only son.

"I will not," Darcy calmly but firmly replied. "I have business to attend to first. I will be home to dine with you this evening." With a shallow bow, he turned on his heel and was gone.

Darcy arrived at the Reid estate in a grim mood. Elizabeth knew immediately that his mother's arrival had not gone well. Once he had greeted everyone, Elizabeth invited him to sit with her at the table, as the household was still at breakfast.

"What has happened?"

"My mother did not come alone," Darcy replied. "She brought the daughter of a friend with her."

Elizabeth's eyes widened and her mouth fell open. "She did? What can she mean by that?"

Darcy waited to reply until a servant had poured him a cup of tea. Then, he took a piece of ham off Elizabeth's plate and popped it in his mouth. When he had chewed and swallowed, he said, "She intends, I believe, to compromise me into marriage." He reached for another piece of meat, but Elizabeth smacked his hand. Instead, he picked up his teacup and took a sip of the flavorful brew.

"Go fix yourself a plate." Elizabeth hit him again when he made another attempt at stealing her breakfast. "Are you serious? She would do that to her own son?"

"My mother will do whatever it takes to reach her objective." Darcy gestured to the footman, quietly saying something to him. When the servant nodded and walked away, Darcy continued, "She tried to insist that my housekeeper put Lady Clarice in the room beside my mother's, which would put her two rooms away from me, as my mother still lives in the mistress' chambers and the master's rooms are beside those."

Elizabeth nodded thoughtfully, not looking at him but clearly listening attentively to every word. "What did you do?" She was increasingly uneasy as she listened to Darcy's report. She bit her lip before tilting her head to look at him.

"I countermanded that order. I had Lady Clarice placed in a guest room on the other side of the house. Mrs. MacIntire knows better than to disobey, and I made that clear to Mother in front of her."

"Good," Elizabeth said, feeling a little of the tension inside release. She watched as the footman brought Darcy a plate of ham and returned to the side of the room to await another summons. "What will you say to her?"

Darcy picked up a piece of his breakfast with his fork as he replied, "I am not certain as of yet. It will largely depend upon what she says to me, though given her behaviour upon her arrival, I cannot see her listening to me right away." Sensing Elizabeth's continued unease, Darcy lowered the fork to his plate. He leaned toward her, and, keeping his free hand under the table, moved it toward her, grasping hers as it lay on her thigh, clutching her skirt. "She cannot separate us," he whispered. "We are married, and no one can change that." Darcy held Elizabeth's hand and watched until he saw her nod, then he let her go and resumed his meal.

Elizabeth swallowed and then picked up her tea. "When is she expecting you back?"

"She did not wish for me to leave in the first place. I told her I would see her at dinner."

Elizabeth set her cup back down, disappointment washing over her that their day was to be shortened. "I see."

Just then, Meg called down the table, "Shall you be here for dinner again, Mr. Darcy?"

Darcy rested his utensil-filled hands beside his plate as he addressed his hostess. "Unfortunately, no, Madam. My mother arrived this morning, just as Mrs. Brodie predicted. I promised to dine with her this evening."

Meg looked at Elizabeth, sympathy in her eyes, as she replied to Darcy. "You must do so, then. I believe we shall *all* miss your company."

"Indeed, we shall," Elizabeth agreed.

Darcy spent the entirety of the day at Briarscraig. He left the estate in the late afternoon with a heavy heart, partially because he had to part with his beloved but also because he knew the conversation he would have with his mother was not going to be pleasant.

Arriving at Glenmoor House, Darcy dismounted and handed off the reins of his horse to a waiting groom. Then, he strode up the short flight of stairs and into the front door, where he handed his hat and gloves to a waiting servant. Darcy stopped to listen for voices, and hearing none, made his way up to his room. He entered, quietly shutting the door behind him, and went straight into his dressing room, where his valet, Smith, was laying out his clothes for the evening.

Darcy wasted no time in questioning his servant. Smith was Darcy's eyes and ears belowstairs, and nothing happened that the valet did not know about. "How did my mother behave today?"

Smith untied the intricate knot of Darcy's cravat while he spoke. "She was demanding, as always. She has quite offended the housekeeper and cook."

Darcy's brows rose as he began to unbutton his waistcoat. "She has already angered Cook?"

"She has. Sent back the tea tray with a message that the ham for the sandwiches was underdone. It was from the same roast that was served for breakfast, and it was not underdone at all."

"No," Darcy murmured. "It was not." He sighed. "What else?"

"She argued with Mrs. MacIntire about Lady Clarice's room, but the housekeeper would not be budged. She told Lady Anne that she had an excellent position and that she was not going to risk losing it to please anyone who was not the master and who she had never laid eyes on before."

"Good. How did Lady Anne react?"

Smith's normally placid and serene expression gave way to pinched lips and rolling eyes. "She grew increasingly loud, insisting upon her own way, until Mrs. MacIntire turned on her heel and left the room. Some of the figurines on the mantel were broken, I am afraid. Lady Anne was in quite a state. Eventually, she charged up the stairs and into her rooms. She and Lady Clarice have been abovestairs all day."

Darcy was amused by his valet's facial expressions. The man had been his personal servant since he finished Cambridge and well knew the whims and fancies of Lady Anne, as well as her temper. "She did not attempt to pry information out of you, did she?"

"She did not. At least, not yet, but I know who *my* employer is, as well. Not a word will pass through my lips about you and your affairs, sir."

"Good. I knew that already, but had to ask. If she had badgered you, I would have had a word with her and insisted she desist."

"Thank you, sir." Smith's lips twitched into a quick smile, then straightened into his normal expression. "There is hot water in the ewer." Bowing, he left Darcy alone to clean himself.

An hour later, Darcy took a deep breath, let it out, and walked into the hallway from his bedchamber. Glancing down the hall, he could see that it was empty and that his mother's door seemed to be shut. Relieved, he strode to the staircase and down to the drawing room, expecting his mother or her guest to be there. He nodded at the footmen and maids as he passed each of them. He had given orders that someone was always to be near, whatever room he was in, and that his bedchamber and dressing room doors were to remain locked at all times. Mrs. MacIntire had taken him at his word about the former, and called grooms in from the stables as though he were hosting a dinner party and needed more people to serve.

Finding the drawing-room empty, Darcy pulled out his watch, noting the time. The housekeeper would soon be announcing the meal, and heaven help them all if Cook's hard work was ruined because the family was late to dine. He spoke to the footman standing just inside the door. "Send a message up to my mother. Tell her we do not hold meals for guests who dally. If we are called in before she gets down here, I will begin eating alone."

The footman nodded, then stepped into the hallway and spoke to another servant. That task complete, he re-entered the drawing room.

Chapter 8

A quarter hour later, Darcy had just stepped toward the dining room when his mother appeared at the top of the staircase, Lady Clarice at her side.

"There you are, Fitzwilliam," Lady Anne called out as she descended the stairs. "I would have a word with you about that housekeeper. Why you got rid of Agnes Hume, I will never understand."

Darcy bowed. "Good evening, Mother, Lady Clarice. Please allow me to escort you to the dining room." He extended his arms for the ladies to take, his expression blank and lips pressed tightly together.

"Did you hear me?" Lady Anne took the proffered arm and allowed Darcy to lead the way down the hall.

"I did hear you. I simply have nothing to say on the matter. Mrs. Hume retired, which is when I replaced her with Mrs. MacIntire, who is old enough and wise enough to run this household the way I wish it to be run. Why you think it should be otherwise is beyond my understanding." When Lady Anne began to fuss once more, Darcy firmly put a stop to it. "No, Mother. Mrs. MacIntire is here to stay. If anyone goes, it shall be you. You may stop trying to order my life for me." He came to a halt just inside the dining room. "I will not be bent to your will," he continued, speaking to Lady Anne. "I am my own man, and master of the estate. I have been an adult for several years now; I do not need instruction on how to live." Darcy bowed to the ladies and strode to the head of the table, leaving the footmen to pull out chairs for them.

For the first part of the meal, Lady Anne was silent. Darcy could clearly see that she was offended, an impression reinforced by the stiff manner in which she held herself. She continued this way as the first course was served, with Lady Clarice choosing to remain quiet, as well. Darcy did not think his mother's guest was angry; rather, she seemed ill at ease, shifting in her seat and darting glances at Lady Anne and himself.

By the time the second course was served, Darcy's mother was prepared to take him on once again. "What this place needs is a mistress, since you will not allow me to manage it. Pemberley, as well, needs a feminine hand to keep it running smoothly. Lady Clarice-."

"Lady Clarice is all that a young gentlewoman ought to be. Yes, Mother, I am aware of your feeling on the matter. However, I have no intentions of marrying her or anyone else of your choosing." Seeing the young lady's eyes grow wide, Darcy apologized to her. "I do not mean to offend, Lady Clarice. However, we would not suit." He paused. "To make it even more clear, you do not suit me. My mother likes to think you do, but she is wrong, just as she was wrong about Lady Charlotte, Lady Beatrice, and Lady Mary."

Lady Clarice flushed, her lips thinning and her eyes flashing. Darcy could see that something he said did not sit well with her, but he was not about to waste time trying to figure out which thing. It was simply not important enough to him, though he did suppose it was rude of him to be so straightforward.

Turning back to his mother, Darcy decided to take the bull by the horns and address her delusion that he would marry where *she* wished. Placing his utensils on his plate, he looked Lady Anne in the eye and spoke. "I will not marry anyone whom my mother has chosen for me. I will marry a lady I have chosen, or I will marry not at all." As Darcy watched his mother's face redden to match Lady Clarice's, he thought of his Elizabeth, whom he had already married. He eagerly anticipated the day they could openly declare their union.

"That is preposterous! It is your duty to obey me, and I demand you do so!"

"I outgrew that duty years ago, Mother." Darcy stood, suddenly enraged at the memory of her treatment of his father, and the way she separated himself from Elizabeth. "I may look like my father, but I am not him. I am my own man, and no one tells me what I may do. You browbeat Papa until he gave in to your wishes, but you will not do the same to me. You will not manipulate me into bending to your will, nor will you force me. And do not think about trying to compromise me with Lady Clarice or anyone else. Should you succeed, the lady will be ruined without salvation, because I will refuse to marry her." Darcy threw his napkin on the table in disgust. "I have suddenly lost my appetite. I want Lady Clarice gone in the morning. If you wish to stay, Mother, I expect better behaviour than you have exhibited to this point. If you cannot behave as a gentlewoman, you may leave, as well." Darcy bowed, then exited the room.

Lady Anne listened in shock as her only son openly rebelled against her authority. She could not believe he had done so. She ground her teeth together, mindful that she was not alone.

Lady Anne turned her gaze on Lady Clarice. Her voice hard and unyielding, she shared the plan that was forming in her mind. "We will set up a compromise. You will go to his chambers, to his bed. He will do the honourable thing."

"But, Lady Anne, he has clearly stated he will not. I am not certain I even wish him for a husband after hearing the words he spoke this evening. He is an arrogant man, not easily led. I have no wish to tie myself to someone I will have to obey at every turn. I am determined to have control over my own life."

"Nonsense. He will turn a blind eye to you, just as his father did to me. The apple does not fall far from the tree. All gentlemen are easily led if one knows how to go about it." With those words, Lady Anne laid out her plan to her newly uncertain accomplice.

A few hours later, Lady Anne was frustrated. She had taken her friend's daughter and led her to Darcy's room, only to find every door locked, including the unused ones. She sent Lady Clarice back to her own chambers, then spent half the night concocting a plan whereby she gained possession of the housekeeper's keys. Lady Anne was determined to see her desires carried out.

It was nearing dawn before Darcy's mother finally fell asleep, exhausted from the thoughts that kept repeating themselves in her mind. After sleeping just four hours, she was up again, determined to visit Elspeth Brodie and find out who Darcy had danced with at the ball.

~~~***~~~

Later that day, Lady Anne settled into a seat beside her old friend, prepared for nice, long visit. "I love what you have done with the place, my dear," she exclaimed, looking around. "It is beautiful!"

Elspeth blushed, but beamed with pleasure. "I had it redone last year, when my Augusta married. It is not every day that one gives away one's only daughter, you know."

"Very true!" Lady Anne shook her head. "I have several more years before Georgiana is old enough to marry, but I do not look forward to giving her up."

"No, I did not, either. It has been a year and I still long to have my little girl back. But, I know that she is happy, and that is the important thing, is it not?"

Lady Anne smiled. "Indeed."

The ladies spent the next quarter hour catching up on each other's news. As the time drew near for the visit to end, Lady Anne brought up the subject about which she most wished to hear. "Tell me about this ball you had. I was happy to hear my son did his duty and danced."

"It was a wonderful time, a true crush! The house was filled to overflowing with guests." Elspeth's hands spoke as much as her words did, gesturing to punctuate her sentences. "Oh, and Fitzwilliam was not shy about dancing, either. So elegant and handsome! I always knew it would be so."

Lady Anne smiled at the description of her son. He had inherited the best combination of her family traits and those of his father. "How many sets did he participate in? Who did he ask?"

Elspeth thought a moment. "I believe he danced with the Millers' daughter before supper. Yes, and then he danced with the niece of that couple from London, the Gardiners. Miss Elizabeth Bennet. I believe he danced with her twice."

Lady Anne had taken a sip of tea as Elspeth was speaking, and upon hearing that her son had danced with the girl she had separated him from, she gasped and choked, spewing tea all over her gown. Quickly, Lady Anne dropped her cup on the table and jumped to her feet. Elspeth joined her with napkins and they brushed and blotted the liquid as best they could. Once they had done fussing, determining that, since Lady Anne was leaving soon and the gown likely ruined anyway, they would finish their discussion. "Elizabeth Bennet? Here, in Scotland? Are you certain, Elspeth?"

Confused by Lady Anne's urgency, Elspeth confirmed it. "She is a lovely young woman, genteel and lively. The Reids think the world of her. Her father owns an estate in Hertfordshire, I believe. Young Darcy was there when I visited a few days ago. I think he is sweet on her." Elspeth smiled. Though she had not married for love, she had come to care deeply for her husband. She was also

89

fond of novels, and had come to believe that all young people should marry for love instead of for convenience or out of necessity.

Lady Anne struggled to keep her countenance. She nodded, hoping her friend noticed nothing amiss. "Excellent news," she lied. Suddenly, she jumped up. "I should be going, I suppose. I am eager to get out of this gown." As Elspeth rose to her feet, Lady Anne grasped her hands. "Thank you for your hospitality. You must come visit Glenmoor before I leave."

Elspeth smiled at her friend. "I will. Thank you for coming." Giving Lady Anne a hug, Elspeth escorted her to the door, waving as the carriage drove away.

As she rode back to Glenmoor, Lady Anne fumed. *I thought I got rid of that chit,* she thought. *How in the world did she show up here? Did someone tell him? He is calling on her! This must stop, and it will stop, if I have to take care of it myself.* With a grim smile, Lady Anne straightened her shoulders. She had taken care of Elizabeth Bennet before, but it had not been a permanent solution. Clearly, sending her away was not going to be enough now, either. This time, she intended to make certain Miss Elizabeth Bennet would never be in Fitzwilliam's path again.

When the carriage came to a stop, Lady Anne flew out of it before the groom got the door all the way open. She stomped up the steps and into the house, tugging off her hat, gloves, and spencer and throwing them at the hapless maid who waited to take them.

Mrs. MacIntire gazed at Lady Anne with wide eyes, wringing her hands at the thought of dealing with the lady when she was in such a state. She did not have long to wonder about possible escapes, for the master's mother barked, "MacIntire, where is my son?"

Curtseying, the housekeeper stiffened her spine and set her face in a stoic expression before replying, "The master went out this morning and has not returned."

Lady Anne huffed, hands on her hips. "Well, where did he go?"

Chapter 9

"I do not know, Madam. He did not say." MacIntire pressed her lips tightly together to hold in her many thoughts. As Lady Anne huffed again, rolling her eyes and turning her head to the side, the housekeeper took the opportunity to inform the master's mother of something else. "Lady Clarice has been awaiting your return, madam. She is in the blue parlour."

Lady Anne nodded. She brushed past the housekeeper and strode down the short hall to the indicated room. She entered, seeing Lady Clarice stand, dressed in travelling clothes. "Where are you going?"

"I have thought about it all night and most of the morning, and have decided," Lady Clarice paused, looking at the floor and taking a deep breath. "I have decided that your son and I would not suit. I know you say his father was easily led, but Mr. Darcy appears to me to be much like my own father—decisive and determined to have his own way. His wealth and status are not enough inducements for me to consider marrying him, even if he were amenable. I will return home; now that you are here and I have explained it all to you, I will call for your carriage to take me and my maid to town. I can hire a footman there to ride with me, and we can begin our trip to London in the morning."

"But, our plans ... surely you do not mean what you say. My son is a catch! He is a wealthy young gentleman in charge of his estate. Your mother and I have long wished for a union between the two of you." Lady Anne tried not to allow her increasing fury to show. She could feel her best-laid plan drifting away.

Lady Clarice shook her head, coming forward to grasp Lady Anne's hands. "I am aware of my mother's hopes and yours. I was willing to go along with you, and to force him to marry me, until I realized what I would be giving up. I have a strong personality, much like yours. I see no evidence that Mr. Darcy would be anything but a strong husband, and that I do not want. I am sorry." Squeezing Lady Anne's hands, Lady Clarice leaned closer and kissed her cheek, then smiled and let go, walking out of the room and calling for the carriage to be brought around.

Lady Anne remained in the parlour, standing stiffly, hands fisted at her sides with her jaw clenched for several long minutes after Lady Clarice departed. Taking deep breaths, she worked to subdue her desire to follow her friend's daughter and demand she stay. It angered Lady Anne beyond bearing to have her plans thwarted. *Well,* she thought, *since I have been unsuccessful in finding an*

*heiress who would marry Fitzwilliam, it is def-
initely time to permanently separate him from
that Bennet chit.* She ground her teeth together and paced the room as she considered and
discarded several ideas for making that separation happen.

Lady Anne was still in a state of high
dudgeon when Darcy returned to the house.
Having heard from Mrs. MacIntire that his
mother had asked after his whereabouts and
what her activities had been while he was
gone, Darcy decided he had best find out what
Lady Anne wanted. Taking a deep breath and
schooling his frown into a mien of indifference, he strode down the hall and into the
blue parlour.

When his mother did not turn at his entrance, Darcy crossed his arms and settled in
to watch her. He could see by the redness of
her countenance and the way she paced back
and forth that she was upset about something
and likely working out a solution to whatever
the problem was. He knew from previous experience that Lady Anne often spoke to herself
when doing so, and if he was patient and quiet, he might learn something.

Unfortunately, such was not the case
this time. His mother walked past him several
times before she made note of his presence,
but she never uttered a word, instead working
out details in her thoughts.

Zoe Burton

"Fitzwilliam! Where have you been?" Lady Anne's hands landed on her hips.

"I was out, Mother." Darcy lowered his arms and bowed from his shoulders. "I trust you enjoyed your day?"

"I suppose I did," Lady Anne countered. "I asked you where you have been all day."

Without showing any of the annoyance that filled his spirit, Darcy reminded his mother that he was his own man. "I am accountable to no one. Where I go and what I do are my business and mine alone."

Lady Anne sputtered in outrage. There ensued a long and heated argument in which she used every manipulative trick she knew to get her son to comply with her wishes, to no avail. Darcy would not be moved from his stance, not even when his mother informed him that she was aware of Elizabeth's presence in the area. Though she threatened and cajoled, implying that she would force Elizabeth to leave just as she had done before, Darcy held firm, telling Lady Anne in no uncertain terms that he was the master and she was the dowager, and that when there was a marriage, it would be to the lady of *his* choosing and no one else's. Eventually, Darcy prevailed, though it was not because his mother gave in. Rather, she quit the room in an angry barrage of words, carrying on all the way to her chambers.

When she was gone, Darcy blew out a breath and lowered his head to his arm, which leaned on the mantel. It had taken every ounce of strength he had to maintain an indifferent expression. *Granted,* he thought, *I did raise my voice a time or two.* Darcy had noticed, though, that his mother seemed to thrive on the times he had let her get the best of him. As soon as he realized that, he leaned against the mantel, behaving for all the world as though he had nothing better to do than to hold up the wall. He had forced himself to breathe before speaking, and to speak in measured tones that conveyed his lack of concern for hers.

Darcy heard a knock on the door and straightened, bidding the knocker to enter. Mrs. MacIntire slipped into the room, curtseying and then standing with head bowed, waiting for permission to speak.

"What is it, MacIntire?"

"If you please, sir, what shall we do about supper?"

Darcy held in a sigh. It would not do to make the housekeeper think he was upset with her. He stared into the fire for just a minute, considering his options. *Too bad I did not stay at Briarscraig with Elizabeth.* He lifted his head and replied to the servant. "I think we shall have trays in our rooms this night."

MacIntire curtseyed with a, "Very good, sir," and scurried away.

Zoe Burton

~~~***~~~

In her chambers, Lady Anne spent a good while pacing back and forth and taking her anger out on the decorations. As always, after a time of screaming and throwing things, she calmed and rang for Ruth. The maid responded promptly, and soon, Lady Anne had her supper tray before her and her bathtub being filled. She hardly tasted her meal, so consumed was she with her thoughts about separating her son from Elizabeth Bennet.

I fear I have tipped my hand, Lady Anne thought. *Fitzwilliam will be on alert for me to confront the chit and her kin.* Lady Anne played with the peas on her plate as she considered her options. *Perhaps I should take some time to consider other methods. My sister has always been the sneakier one of us. If she were here, she could best advise me, but since she is not, I must rely on myself and my own intelligence to achieve my goal.*

She finally set aside the remnants of her beef pie and marched into the dressing room to soak in the hot bath. Then, having decided to bide her time and act with forethought instead of immediacy, Lady Anne went to bed early, falling asleep swiftly and soundly.

~~~***~~~

The next week passed much as the previous one had, with Darcy making long visits to the Reid home and his mother making visits to and receiving them from various neighbors.

Darcy and Elizabeth managed to find some time alone every day, though generally not long enough to more than kiss. They were frustrated by this, but knew that the situation they were in would not last long.

"Your aunt and uncle are dropping you off in Kent on the way home?" Darcy asked as he and Elizabeth strolled the far end of the gardens two days before she was scheduled to leave.

"Yes," Elizabeth confirmed. "It will be a bit out of the way, but they do not mind. They will be assured of my safety if I am travelling with them instead of alone or with a hired companion."

"I will feel better, as well. I do not like the thought of my wife riding in a post carriage." Darcy caressed Elizabeth's hand as it rested on his arm.

Elizabeth sighed. She and Darcy had discussed this before. All she said, though, was, "I know." She was tired of soothing him on this issue and wanted the subject changed. "Your mother has yet to visit Mrs. Reid."

Darcy did not reply immediately, his thoughts going to Lady Anne and his curiosity as to her activities and plans. "I wondered about that. Is Mrs. Reid distressed?"

"I cannot say. She is always so cheerful; it is difficult to discern her true feelings. I would guess that she is at least curious as to why Lady Anne seems to be avoiding her. I could tell her, I suppose, that it is likely my fault." Elizabeth shrugged.

"You could, but only if you wish to explain our history to her." Darcy squeezed Elizabeth's hand, tilting his head to see her expression.

"Yes, and that might lead to other questions that we have agreed not to reveal the answers to." Elizabeth glanced up at Darcy, her eyebrow raised.

"True." Darcy was quiet for a few minutes, leading Elizabeth to their favorite place of secrecy and guiding her inside. When they had reached the bench in the centre and arranged themselves upon it, he continued. "I do not understand the reason for it, but I am happy you will be leaving the day after tomorrow. I feel as though there is some unnamed danger lurking about." He played with the ribbons of her bonnet, his brow creased. Biting his lip, he looked into her eyes. "It is ...," his eyes wandered up and down the wall of green that faced them and then sighed deeply. "I do not know what the feeling is or how to describe it, nor can I identify the source of the danger. Unsettled is how I would describe it, I suppose."

Elizabeth had watched Darcy's expression carefully, her own brow creasing to match his. When he had finished speaking, she brought a hand from his shoulder to caress his cheek and the soft hair of his side whiskers. "Are you worried about a danger to me?"

"Yes, I am." The crease between Darcy's eyebrows grew even deeper, and lines appeared to bracket his lips as a frown formed on his face. "I wish I knew the source. The only occurrence that is different now from what it was a few days ago is that my mother is here."

"Perhaps you are worried that she will come to Briarscraig and do what she did in Derbyshire four years ago."

"That is possible." Darcy paused. "Well, there is nothing I can do about it, since I do not know the origin of it. I wish I could travel with you to Hunsford, but if I do, my aunt will hear of it. That we do not want."

"You will come to Kent, though?"

"Oh, yes. I will most certainly do so, as soon as possible. It may take a few days; I will probably escort Mother to London first. Then, I promised to visit a friend in Cambridge for a few days. From there, I will go directly to Rosings."

"Will your mother not tell her sister about me? I am quite certain that my cousin Collins will have already told his 'esteemed patroness' my name." Elizabeth could not hide the sarcasm in her voice as she mimicked her cousin's manner.

Darcy laughed at his wife's antics. "Mother and Lady Catherine do not correspond regularly, which is odd given that they are so much alike. They both are fond of ordering the lives of those around them, and I suspect they do it to each other, as well, and end up resentful of each other."

"So to preserve family harmony, they avoid each other?" Elizabeth giggled at the thought.

"It seems that way," Darcy replied with a chuckle. "We should be safe enough there. And," he continued, this time whispering in Elizabeth's ear, "There are many very *private* places for us to meet at Rosings."

Grinning, Elizabeth whispered in Darcy's ear, "I can hardly wait," before capturing his lips in a passionate kiss.

Chapter 10

Upon his return to Glenmoor, Darcy was surprised to find that his mother was not there. According to the housekeeper, Lady Anne had been invited to stay for dinner at a neighboring estate and had sent word that she would be gone most of the evening. Relieved to be free of her oppressive company for a night, Darcy strolled into a little-used parlour in the back of the house, intending to read for a while.

The room he had chosen was small, and decorated in an older style. *It could use a refreshing*, Darcy thought to himself as he took in the faded curtains, rug, and upholstery. He considered going to the library for the evening, but the big chair by the window looked comfortable, and the room had a small fire already lit, which the library did not. Shrugging, he rang the bell, informing the footman who responded that he would take his evening meal on a tray in this room and asking for a lamp to be lit on the table so he could better see to read, and then settled himself into the chair.

As he arranged himself for maximum comfort, Darcy felt something hard poke at his backside. Standing, he laid his book on the table and turned, bending over the chair and sliding his hand between the seat cushion and the back. He found the hard object and pulled it out, surprised to see a book. He turned around again and resumed his seat, opening the small tome. Darcy's brows shot up when he realized the book was, in fact, a journal. "This is someone's private thoughts. I wonder whose it is and how long it has been here," he murmured, beginning to read.

February 1, 1800

I am shaking with fury. See how the strokes of my pen wobble? Not at all how my words usually look.

What has me in such a state? One of the upstairs maids broke a priceless vase that my grandfather bought for my grandmother long ago. It was a family heirloom and that lazy girl was careless with it.

I have disciplined her. I was careful to leave no marks where they can be seen, and I made sure she understood that relating to anyone what has happened to her will result in her dismissal without a reference. George has some fanciful ideas about how to treat servants, as though they were equals. They must have come from his upbringing. After all, I married below me, for all that the Darcys are fabulously wealthy. We among the peerage have higher ways than anyone else.

May 31, 1807

The deed is done. The process was much slower than I anticipated, but in the end, a fall from one of his hunters finished him off. It honestly amazes me that no one seemed to notice the oddities of his recent appearance and behavior. But, I will not complain, because that is a blessing and a boon to me. If anyone knew, I would hang, but no one will know. Not now and not ever.

August 15, 1808

I took care of a problem today. A few bits of hemlock in the tea and a suggestion to the maid that she taste it because it did not seem quite right to me and the deed was done. One less obstacle in my way. She was a liability that had to be taken care of. If anyone ever connects me to George's death, it will all be over for me. I can promise you, that will never happen.

By the time his supper arrived, Darcy was no longer certain he was hungry. The contents of the journal he had found were alarming; even more so was his realization of the author. He leaned back in the chair, his mind whirling, as the maid and footman laid out his meal. His heart raced to match the speed of his thoughts. He feared he might cast up his accounts. *What am I to do? Should I tell anyone? Certainly, I must warn Gardiner to be on alert as he travels. I do not know what Mother is not capable of!*

The footman had brought a decanter of port, placing it on a separate table nearer to the fire, in anticipation that the master would request it after he ate. Darcy rose from the chair and strode to the port as soon as the servants vacated the room. With shaking hands, he poured a glass of the wine, bringing it to his lips and gulping half of it at once. He refilled the glass and took it back to the table by the window. Forcing himself to eat, Darcy picked at the meal, his thoughts still consumed by the problem at hand.

After a half-hour of contemplation and worry, Darcy rang the bell again, this time instructing the footman to clear the remains of his meal and to have paper and ink brought in. While he waited for the writing supplies, he mentally composed the letter he intended to write. Finally, pen in hand, he was able to begin.

July 2, 1810

Glenmoor, Scotland

Dear Cousin,

I hope this letter finds you well and that your recruits have not plagued you overly much since we last spoke. Everyone here is well. Mother showed up a few days ago. Apparently, a neighbor wrote her about me and she ran up here to supervise me. I do not have to tell you how I reacted to that.

My purpose in writing is not one that I am comfortable with, but I feel that you—and probably your father—need to know of it. Mother is currently dining out at the home of a neighbour. In her absence, I chose to read in a room I do not usually inhabit. Without going into the boring details, I found a journal tucked into the chair where I sat. It was my mother's, and I do not know how to say this, I truly do not. Instead, I will ask a favour of you. Please do go to my uncle and ask him about my father's death. As you know, I was away at the time, and was told that he had been thrown from his horse. Was there anything else to it? I desperately need to know.

Zoe Burton

I will be in London in a week or so. I intend to bring Mother with me and hope to speak to you and the earl while I am there. I hope you can find a way to be free for an evening at that time.

Your devoted cousin,

FD

Darcy reread his missive, making corrections here and there, and then writing out a clean copy. This he sealed, writing the direction on the outside. Crumpling the first draft, he tossed it in the fire, watching as it burned. He picked up his book and the letter and refilled his glass, then strode out of the room. He gave the note to the first footman he found, requesting that a trustworthy groom be found to carry it to London at first light. Then, he went to his rooms. He readied himself for bed and got under the covers. He tossed and turned all night, plagued with nightmares.

When morning came and his valet woke him up, Darcy dragged himself out of bed, exhausted but determined to warn his Elizabeth and her family to be extra cautious.

In the dressing room, Darcy could see Smith look him up and down out of the corner of his eye. He was not surprised when the valet asked if he should ring for coffee to be brought up.

"Yes, do," Darcy replied to the request. "I require something this morning to wake me up."

Smith did as was requested and then returned to shave Darcy. "Are you well, sir?"

Darcy opened one eye, his head leaned back against the chair. "I did not sleep well." Closing the orb once more, Darcy stifled a yawn. "I had nightmares. Strange ones." He shuddered. "I hope they are never repeated."

Smith remained silent while he shaved his master. After he handed Darcy a towel with which to dry his face, the valet spoke again. "Some believe our dreams are manifestations of our thoughts."

Darcy handed the towel back. His eyes were set afar off, staring unseeingly at the dresser before him. "I suppose that is true in this case. However," he looked at Smith, "I will not allow what I saw in my mind last night to be what happens today." Rising from the chair, Darcy began to dress, now and then sipping the coffee that had arrived while he was being shaved. When he finished, he examined himself in the pier glass. Tugging on his waistcoat, he nodded. "Excellent work, as usual, Smith. I am going to Briarscraig, but my mother is not to know this. I know you always do, but keep a very close eye and ear to what goes on here today, especially to what is said. We will leave for London in the morning."

"Very good, sir." Smith bowed and watched Darcy walk away.

A short while later, Darcy was announced at Briarscraig, where the whole party had recently quit the breakfast parlour.

"I missed you this morning. I did not know what to do with myself when I was not required to defend my plate from your attack." Elizabeth's tease was accompanied by a raised brow. She was clearly attempting to suppress a smirk but failing spectacularly.

Darcy's worried spirit was eased by his beloved's lively impertinence. He kissed her hand as he bowed over it. "I apologize for keeping my lady waiting. Were you able to take sustenance, or was your appetite depressed by my absence and the accompanying lack of activity?" He winked.

Elizabeth laughed, her free hand coming up to cover her mouth. "You, Mr. Darcy, are learning to tease! Who would have thought it possible?" She brought her hand down to lay atop his, which still held her fingers in its grasp.

"I needed the correct teacher to instruct me. You have done very well with that." Darcy started to lean down to kiss his wife's smiling lips but caught himself just in time. Instead, he grinned at her, squeezing her hand.

"You have been a very capable student." Elizabeth stared at Darcy, her smile glued to her face, willing his mouth closer. When he clutched her digits tighter, she was startled out of her thoughts. Blushing, she squeezed back.

"I, for one, am happy to see you, Mr. Darcy, because Elizabeth has been quite dull this morning without you." Maddie winked at her niece, laughing to herself when Elizabeth blushed. "Please sit, sir."

Darcy did as Maddie invited him to, settling down on the couch beside his beloved and clasping his hands in his lap to keep them from reaching for Elizabeth's.

Elizabeth tilted her head, examining Darcy carefully. He seemed distracted today, and while she had never been one to demand to be the centre of anyone's attention, the dark circles under his eyes made her wonder if he had something on his mind. "Are you well?" she asked.

Darcy nodded, turning in the seat so he faced Elizabeth. "I am. I am only tired. My dreams last night were not the good ones I have become accustomed to having." He smiled at her again, hoping to hide the extent of his discomfort but knowing his perceptive Elizabeth would probably see through it.

"I see," Elizabeth replied, nodding slowly, her sharpened gaze taking him in. After a moment of contemplation, she asked another question, this one softly and for his ears only. "What was the cause of your bad dreams?"

Darcy shifted uncomfortably and glanced at the Reids and Gardiners, on the

111

other side of the seating area. He blew out a breath before he answered her. "I found something disturbing last evening. A book. The stories within were ... alarming. They were nothing that I should have been reading at that time of day."

Elizabeth's eyebrows rose high up on her forehead. "Indeed?" It was unlike Darcy to be missish, and she could not help but wonder at this book he described.

Darcy glanced out the window. The always-grey sky was covered with darker than usual clouds, and he could see that it would rain at some point during the day. Still, he needed to speak to Elizabeth in private, and a walk in the gardens was his best option for that. Looking back at Elizabeth, he asked her opinion.

"I think that is a wonderful idea." Elizabeth clasped her hands together and turned her gaze to her aunt, uncle, and friends. "What say you?"

"I would enjoy a stroll," Maddie affirmed, setting aside her embroidery. "Edward, Meg?"

"I am afraid I must decline," Meg demurred. "I must meet with my housekeeper and then reconcile my accounts." She grimaced. "Hardly my favorite thing to do, and not what I would wish to do, but I have put it off long enough. My dear husband is becoming impatient with me; he wishes to hear my

report on the state of our household finances."
Meg grinned at Reid.

"Indeed, I do. The Good Book commands us to know the state of our flocks. It is not wise to let that go too long." Gerald's words were stern, but the twinkle in his eye let his listeners know he was not angry. He held out a hand to his wife to help her rise.

"I am afraid I must also decline," Edward informed the group. "Reid and I have some final details to review to wrap up our business. I trust Maddie will be able to keep our two young lovers on the straight and narrow." He smirked.

Maddie rolled her eyes as he stood. "Perhaps I will allow them to wander all the way to Gretna Green without me." She sniffed. "Of course, I can keep them out of mischief."

Everyone laughed at that, and parted ways. Within a few minutes, Darcy and Elizabeth were wandering the meandering paths in the shrubbery in silence. Darcy was working out in his mind how to tell Elizabeth what he had read, and Elizabeth was planning how she would pry out of Darcy the details of his nightmares.

When they reached the center of the labyrinth, Darcy sat on the bench and pulled Elizabeth into his lap. Immediately, they kissed, a long, passionate exchange. When both were left breathless and panting, they separated. They held each other tightly as they calmed. Finally, Elizabeth pulled back, framing his face in her hands. Kissing his lips softly once more, she pleaded with him, "Tell me what is wrong. What was in that book that caused the steadiest gentleman I know to have nightmares?"

Chapter 11

Darcy looked at his secret wife, allowing his eyes to roam her sweet features. When he had his words ordered in his mind, he looked down, took one of her hands in his free one, and began.

"I found a journal." Darcy spoke haltingly as he tried to explain it to Elizabeth without frightening her. "It was full of ... it was filled with the exploits of the writer, things that she had done to others. Actions she had taken against people who angered her or got in the way of what she wanted."

Elizabeth's eyes had grown large when Darcy began referring to the author of the journal as "she." "I am almost afraid to ask, though I suspect I know the answer already. Whose journal was it?"

Darcy looked Elizabeth in the eye. "It was my mother's."

Elizabeth's mouth fell open. She quickly shut it, then opened it again to say, "I suspected it was hers, but hoped it was not. What kind of actions did she write about?" She squeezed Darcy's hand.

Darcy sighed. "I would rather not tell you, but I know that you will hound me until I do."

Elizabeth pursed her lips and cocked her brow at him. "I will, so you had better tell me and be done with it."

Shaking his head, Darcy rolled his eyes but began to share with Elizabeth the things he had read. "The diary covered probably a decade of events. She does not write in it often, it seems. She described ruining the lives of maids and footmen who told my father tales of her behavior with them. I gathered that she beats servants on occasion, which is something my father would never have condoned. She wrote of you, and how she sent me away and carried on until you left, as well. She also wrote of poison. In looking at the dates of the two or three entries there, I begin to suspect that my father did not die the way I was told he did."

Elizabeth was silent for a long moment, her hand over her mouth and her brows raised to her hairline. "When was her latest entry? What did it say? Surely she would have been writing in it here in Scotland for you to have found it."

With a deep sigh, Darcy confessed. "She had written of you again, and how she intends to 'permanently separate' you from me."

"Permanently?" Elizabeth went white at the implications. "What can we do?"

"As you are leaving tomorrow, I am hoping you will remain safe from her. As I said, she only rarely corresponds with my aunt and is not aware that you are going to Hunsford. She will not know where you are, only that you have left Scotland. I do plan to insist that your uncle travel with an armed guard. I will pay for it myself if I have to." Darcy pulled Elizabeth tighter to him with the hand that rested at her waist. "I will take her to London as planned, and then come to you in Kent in a couple weeks."

Elizabeth sighed. "I will feel safer with a guard, thank you. How will you explain the need to my uncle? Will you tell him all? He might want to separate us himself if he knows your mother is a danger to me."

"I hope that what we have already told him is enough for him to acquiesce to my wishes. Regardless of his decision, whether he accepts or not, an armed guard will travel with you, even if they must do it at a distance. It is my duty to keep you safe, and I intend to do so." Darcy leaned in for a soft, gentle kiss. "I love you too much to leave you in danger."

Elizabeth smiled at Darcy, lifting her hand once more, this time to stroke his cheek. "You are the best gentleman I have ever met. I love you, too. I am so proud and happy to be your wife." She leaned her forehead against his, and soon they were kissing again.

Darcy ended up spending the night at Briarscraig when, just before the evening meal, the skies opened.

"It will be impossible for you to travel in this deluge, Darcy. You had best stay here, even if it means you get a late start tomorrow." Reid looked at his neighbor in concern.

Darcy, who had glanced out the window with everyone else when the rain started pounding on it, agreed. "I believe you are correct. It will not be too much of an imposition?"

"Not at all!" Reid glanced at Elizabeth and then turned his focus back to Darcy. "I am quite certain there are those among us who would greatly enjoy having your company for a few hours more today."

Darcy had caught his host's look and saw Elizabeth blush at the gentleman's words. "Since I will equally enjoy more time at Briarscraig, I will accept your invitation. Thank you."

"Will your mother worry? Should you send a note?" Meg chewed her lip. She would certainly be concerned if one of her children did not come home after visiting the neighbors.

"That will not be necessary. Lady Anne and I are accustomed to living apart. She will assume I stayed here and will not worry unless I do not appear in the morning." Darcy always found it difficult to speak of his mother, but with his new-found knowledge of her activities, it was even harder.

With a nod, Meg accepted Darcy's explanation and resumed her needlework. A few quick minutes later, a servant announced dinner and Darcy escorted Elizabeth to the dining room.

That night after the house grew quiet, Darcy sneaked into Elizabeth's bedchamber, where the pair of them enjoyed the fruits of their secret marriage until nearly dawn.

~~~***~~~

Darcy and Elizabeth stood beside the Gardiners' carriage, saying goodbye for the second time. Though the first had been full of kisses and tears, this one was more subdued.

"I will see you soon, I promise." Darcy squeezed Elizabeth's hands.

"No more than a fortnight?"

"No more than a fortnight; sooner if I can." Darcy's arms ached with the need to pull Elizabeth close. He fought the impulse, but only because there were so many people in sight of them.

Elizabeth gripped Darcy's hands tightly. She longed with everything in her to run her fingers across his brow and smooth away the lines that grew deeper with every passing second. She glanced over his shoulder, seeing her aunt descending the front steps. Looking back at Darcy, she whispered, "I love you."

"I love you, too," Darcy murmured back, lifting Elizabeth's hands and kissing the backs before letting them go.

Maddie paused beside the couple. "Well, Lizzy, are you looking forward to our travels? I know how much you enjoy seeing new places." She glanced at Darcy, and then, a smirk lifting the corner of her mouth, added, "Perhaps this time, the scenery you *wish* to see is not going to be there?"

Elizabeth blushed, but the corners of her lips lifted in a pale imitation of her usual engaging smile. "I believe you are right, Aunt."

Just then, Gardiner joined them, their host and hostess behind him. "Are we ready?" He rubbed his hands together with a grin.

"Yes," Elizabeth sighed. "I suppose we are." She looked at Darcy again, her heart aching at leaving him.

"All will be well. I will see you again, I promise." Darcy kissed Elizabeth's hand one last time before handing her into the carriage. He waited while Gardiner performed the same courtesy for Maddie and then spoke. "Thank you for agreeing to the outriders. I will feel better knowing they are with you."

Gardiner clapped his hand on the younger man's shoulder, leaving it rest there. "You are welcome. I know Maddie appreciates it, as well. I will not press you about your reasons for insisting. However, there are enough dangers on the roads that we will all feel better for having extra men."

"I know I probably seem overprotective, but there are reasons for my caution. I cannot explain them now, but I promise I will later. Thank you, Gardiner; please take care, and take care of Miss Elizabeth."

Gardiner slapped Darcy's shoulder again, then turned and boarded the carriage. Darcy watched as the equipage drove off, waving at Elizabeth, whose face was pressed to the window. Soon, they were out of sight. Darcy turned, farewelled his hosts, and mounted his horse, making his way back to Glenmoor.

Darcy and his mother did not leave that day as planned. Lady Anne, upon hearing of Elizabeth's departure, decided a visit to Briarscraig was in order. Remembering her desire to proceed with caution, and seeing that the chit was gone, Lady Anne kept quiet on the subject of Darcy and Elizabeth. She quietly seethed inside whenever their supposed attachment was mentioned. She was very happy, indeed, to learn that no announcement had been made. According to Meg Reid, the pair was clearly attached but surprisingly, not betrothed.

~~~***~~~

The next day, Lady Anne and Darcy began their own trip south to London. Darcy was relieved that Elizabeth had a day's head start. He worried less about trouble, knowing they would not cross paths.

Travelling with Lady Anne was always a trial for Darcy. His mother was presumptuous and harsh, and their conversations always left him angry. The mere thought of a week trapped in a confined carriage with her was enough to make his head ache.

By distracting himself with thoughts of Elizabeth, and by keeping his nose in a book as much as possible, the trip passed far more quickly than he thought it would. Soon, they were stopping in front of Darcy House and disembarking. Darcy had never been so happy to be home!

For Lady Anne, the trip was equally uncomfortable, largely because her stubborn son ignored her. Eventually, she gave up trying to speak to him. The effort was exhausting, and her energy was better spent contemplating the situation with Elizabeth Bennet.

Lady Anne had at first been ecstatic that Darcy had voluntarily separated himself from the chit. The more she thought about it, though, the more uncertain she became. She heard the words of her neighbors in her head, repeatedly, telling her that Darcy and Elizabeth had clearly developed an attachment. Meg Reid had claimed that he was a constant visitor at Briarscraig and had expressed surprise that no announcement had been made.

Lady Anne looked across the carriage to her son, who was reading again. His behaviour toward and in the presence of Lady

Clarice was a clear indication that he did not care about his mother's wishes and opinions. *But, he would not have parted from that girl if he were attached, would he?* Lady Anne chewed her lip. *No, not unless he knew he would see her again soon. I wonder if he plans to elope. He would not do it from London, surely, not when he was right there in Scotland, within a mile of a church.* Lady Anne's eyes widened, and she sat perfectly straight, still, and stiff as a thought entered her mind. *He could not have!* Her sharp gaze narrowed on Darcy. *He will not admit to it if I ask, I think. If he has married her, there is a reason he is hiding it. As soon as we arrive in London, I will begin investigating this. If they are married, steps must be taken to remove Elizabeth Bennet from this world. I will not give up my place as mistress of Pemberley to a low-born fortune hunter!*

Lady Anne spent the rest of the trip planning her next moves.

Chapter 12

True to his word, Darcy arrived at Rosings in Kent a fortnight after Elizabeth left Scotland. As his carriage passed the parsonage at Hunsford, he noted a tall, heavy man in a cleric's collar bowing at his equipage. *That must be Elizabeth's cousin*, he thought. *He certainly seems odd. Perhaps he is as ridiculous as she claims he is.*

Though Darcy's eyes searched the area around the parsonage and the paths he passed, he did not see his Elizabeth. He was disappointed, but since they had already planned to meet the morning after his arrival, he was not distressed. There would be plenty of time to spend with his wife during this visit.

Almost before he knew it, Darcy's coach and four pulled up in front of his aunt's house. He took the couple of minutes between the time the equipage came to a stop and the groom opened the door to gird himself for the coming nosiness of Lady Catherine De Bourgh. When the portal opened, he blew out a breath, stiffened his spine, and descended to the gravel drive. Taking time to settle his top hat more firmly on his head, he inhaled once more, let it out, and headed into the grand home, his mask of indifference firmly in place.

"Welcome to Rosings, Mr. Darcy. I trust you had a pleasant trip," Lady Catherine's butler greeted in a solemn tone.

"Thank you, Winters, I did." Darcy handed the servant his hat and gloves. "Is my aunt in the throne room?"

A twinkle appeared in the butler's eye at Darcy's description of the formal drawing room, though his stoic demeanour did not change. "She is. Follow me, please."

Darcy did as directed, though it chafed at him. His aunt was a stickler for propriety, even with family and in situations that should have been informal. As he glanced around at the gilded and gaudy décor that had not changed for as long as he could remember, it did not surprise him that Lady Catherine should be so. *She does like to throw her rank about,* he thought.

"Mr. Darcy, Madam." Winters announced Darcy in his deep monotone and then bowed and allowed the gentleman to pass him. Darcy could swear he saw, out of the corner of his eye, the butler's mouth twitch as though he wanted to smile. He knew Winters was amused and appreciated his dry sense of humour. Heaven knew, someone at Rosings needed some.

"You are late, Nephew." Lady Catherine's strident and demanding voice carried from the far end of the room. She remained seated in her large and ornate chair, the one

Darcy and his cousins had dubbed "the throne" as children.

Not willing to shout from afar, as his mother's sister obviously was, Darcy strode deeper into the large room. Finally reaching the seating area where Lady Catherine's favorite seat was located, he bowed to her and to his cousin, Anne, who sat on a settee to the right of her mother's chair. "I am not late, Aunt. I have arrived at exactly the time I told you I would." He pulled his watch out of his waistcoat pocket and opened it, making note of the time. "As a matter of fact, I am a full quarter hour early."

Lady Catherine's mouth turned down at the corners. She sniffed then, and with her chin, gestured to the empty space on the settee beside her daughter. "Sit down. It gives me the headache to lean back and look up at you."

Darcy did sit, but not where he had been instructed to. "How have you and my cousin fared, Aunt? I hope the summer heat was not too much for you."

"We have been well. We expected you much earlier."

Darcy sighed to himself. Clearly, Lady Catherine was spoiling for a fight. Recalling the manner in which his father and his Uncle Matlock had always dealt with her, Darcy was again direct. "I cannot imagine why you would, when I wrote with specific details. I am

Zoe Burton

not to blame if you cannot read a simple letter or tell time properly."

Again, his aunt sniffed. She eyed him up and down out of the corner of her eye, her lips compressed tightly. "Every time you visit, you sound more like your father."

Darcy shrugged. "I do not know that I do or do not, though I strive to emulate his good qualities. I will take your comment as a compliment and thank you, though. Nothing would make me happier than to be a replica of such a good and esteemed gentleman."

"Anne has awaited your visit with in-creasing anticipation, have you not, Daughter?"

Anne, who was of a sickly constitution, lifted a cloth to her nose to dab at it and then replied, "Indeed." Her voice was clear but spoke the words in a monotone that left the hearer uncertain as to her true feelings on the matter.

With a crisp nod and her chin lifted high, Lady Catherine turned from her daughter to her nephew. "Your own attachment to us, to Rosings, grows with every visit. I watched you as you entered this room. You admire it just as we do. It awaits you as its master. When you and Anne marry, I will turn over the running of the place to you completely."

Darcy stood, his nostrils flaring. "Lady Catherine. I have told you repeatedly that I do not intend to marry my cousin. My father told you the same, long ago, and I know the earl

128

has confirmed it more than once." He held up a hand, palm out, when Lady Catherine began to bluster. "No, Aunt. I do not want to hear how you and my mother desire it, nor do I want to listen again to how the pair of you planned the union when Anne and I were in our cradles.

"For one thing, Anne is three years younger, and I was already walking when she was born. We were never in cradles at the same time. For another thing, regardless of what you and Mother wish, my marriage is my business and mine alone. I know my duty, and I have never given anyone, not my parents, not my sister, not anyone in the family, reason to doubt my intentions or my honour. Cease and desist this nonsense now, or I will leave forthwith."

Lady Catherine had stood when Darcy began his speech and now remained on her feet, her lips pinched into a tight ball, breathing harshly through her nose. She knew he was correct; her brothers had both told her in no uncertain terms that Darcy would marry where he would, and that his choice would never be her daughter. Still, she knew if she threw her weight around a bit, the gentlemen in her life always gave in, eventually. That Darcy was now so firmly standing his ground made her very unhappy. She feared that if she pushed him, he might leave, and that she did not want. She might still be able to work on him if he stayed. So, as much as she wished to rail at him, she forced an apology past her clenched jaw. "I apologize. You are correct. Forgive me for attempting to force the matter."

Darcy nodded sharply. "You are forgiven, but do not let it happen again. I will go to my room now and refresh myself. I will see you at dinner." Bowing first to his aunt and then to his cousin, Darcy turned on his heel and departed, striding out the door and up the stairs. Smith waited on the landing and Darcy addressed him. "Did she put me in the usual suite of rooms?"

"Yes, sir. Water for a bath is on the way up and I have ordered tea."

"Good. I am in dire need of both." Without another word, he made his way down the corridor and around the corner to the chambers he always occupied when he was at Rosings.

As he stripped his clothing away a few minutes later, he asked Smith if he had heard any news since his arrival.

"I did. It seems Lady Catherine's rector's wife has a friend visiting."

Darcy smiled. "Does she?"

"She does." Smith allowed a smirk to lift one corner of his lips for just a brief moment. "Word is that this young lady can hold her own against Lady Catherine."

Now, Darcy grinned. That sounded like his Elizabeth. "How does my aunt feel about this?"

"The servants cannot seem to decide if she likes the young lady or not. Some feel that she admires her spunk, but others are certain she dislikes the impertinence."

"Hm, well, I suppose it could go either way."

"Indeed, it could, sir. You will have to watch and see."

With a chuckle, Darcy stepped into the tub, sinking down into the hot water and allowing it to relax him. Smith wandered in and out, laying out shaving items and clothing, and then rinsing Darcy after he had finished washing his hair and bathing. Once the water cooled, Darcy rose and stepped out of the tub, using the towel that sat on a nearby stool to dry himself and then donning a robe. As he dressed with Smith's assistance, he addressed the valet on a matter he had kept silent about before.

"You know that I spent much of my time in Scotland at a neighboring estate."

"Yes, sir."

"I am telling you this now, even though I suspect you had it figured out long ago. Do you recall the young lady I was planning to propose to at Pemberley, right before my tour of the Kingdom?"

Smith thought a moment, but only because he was uncertain about the lady's name. "I do remember it. You were distraught to be separated from her. I believe her name was Miss Elizabeth, or something like that?"

"Yes, Elizabeth. Do you remember the reason for our separation?"

"Oh, yes. Your mother."

Darcy nodded. "Miss Elizabeth Bennet was visiting the estate I spent my time at in Scotland."

"I thought that was her! You had the same sense of contentment at Glenmoor that you had at Pemberley when I first came into your service."

"There is more. This is a secret you must guard with your life."

Smith became somber at once. "You may depend upon me, Mr. Darcy."

"I know I can. I only wish to remind you, because if word of this gets out, Elizabeth's life could be in danger. I married Miss Bennet at Gretna Green the night before the ball at Briarscraig."

Smith had known about the late night ride his master had taken but had not known the purpose of it. He hid his surprise quite well. His professionalism was the reason Darcy trusted him implicitly.

"Congratulations, sir." Smith bowed, and then tied Darcy's cravat.

"Thank you. There is more. While at Glenmoor, I found a journal of my mother's that contained some very disturbing things. If she gets word that Elizabeth is here, she will waste no time in coming here, and her journal indicates a desire to get rid of my wife in a manner from which there is no return." Darcy raised his brow as he looked his valet in the eye. "No one must know that Elizabeth and I are married. I intend to see as much of her as I can, and have planned out some assignations. I will require your assistance to set them up and to keep nosy servants from realizing what is happening."

"Very good, sir. I look forward to thwarting their plans to keep their mistress informed of your activity." Smith stood with his hands clasped in front of him. His eyes crinkled the slightest bit, the only outward indication of his amusement.

Darcy chuckled. "That is good to hear." He examined himself in the mirror and nodded at the perfection of his attire.

"Will you be seeing Mrs. Darcy this evening?"

"I doubt it; my aunt rarely invites guests in the first night a family member is in residence. I will see my wife in the morning, however. Lay out my riding clothes. Then, I will need a meal packed. I plan to be out most of the morning." Darcy paused for a moment as he went through his list in his mind. "Make certain there is enough food for two, and a bottle of wine. Take a blanket and two cups to the folly and leave them inside." He stopped again, tapping his lip with his finger. Then, deciding that he had covered all possibilities brought his hand down to his side. "That should cover it. We will speak of it again in the morning."

"Yes, sir." Smith bowed and waited while Darcy left the chamber. Then, after examining the state of the room and not seeing anything that was out of place, he followed his master out the door.

Chapter 13

The next morning, Darcy set out early for his ride. He took a circuitous route around the home farm, ending at a pretty grove of trees near a folly. A long time ago, his aunt had insisted on having the structure added to the property, though she rarely visited it. It had been years since the last time she had driven out this way, preferring to remain close to home.

Before he left Scotland, Darcy had given Elizabeth directions to this place and, just as he expected, by the time he arrived, she was standing on the porch, waiting for him. He observed her excited clapping of hands and the grin on her face with a joy that was unmatched in his experience. Not even finding her again after four long years had come close; that moment had been tinged with the fear that she had stopped loving him or, worse, had married another. This time, Darcy saw his beloved with the full knowledge that she was his forever.

Darcy pulled his mount to a stop beside the small building and leapt off. He heard Elizabeth squeal and dropped the reins, holding out his arms to catch her. She threw herself into his embrace, wrapping her arms around his neck. Darcy staggered back under the force of her motion, but hugged her tightly to him. He set her down and then captured her lips in a deep and passionate kiss.

Many long, breathless minutes later, the couple pulled apart. Their embrace changed from passionate to tender, and they held each other close, murmuring words of love.

"I have missed you," Elizabeth whispered into Darcy's coat. "I have never lived through such a long fortnight in my life. I thought you would never arrive!"

Darcy kissed Elizabeth's bonnet-covered head. "I missed you, as well. And, I agree that it was the longest fortnight I have ever experienced." He squeezed her form, feeling an unexpected relief at having her molded to his body. He ran his hands up and down her back for a while and then, kissing her head once more, stepped back. His hands slid down her arms to her hands and he grasped them tightly. Looking in her eyes, he caught his breath at the love that shone in her mien. He leaned down to kiss her softly, but forced himself to stop before he did more. Standing upright again, he spoke around the lump of joy that had lodged in his throat. "I brought us a picnic."

"A picnic? At this time of day?" Elizabeth laughed. "What a lovely idea! Have you a blanket? Where shall we spread it out?"

"It should be here," Darcy nodded at the building beside them, "inside the folly, if my man followed directions and did not run into trouble."

"Well then, let us go look." Elizabeth tucked her hand under Darcy's elbow and grinned. She allowed him to lead her back up to the porch and around to the folly's door.

Darcy let go of his Elizabeth's hand so he could open the latch and push the door. He was happy to note that Smith had come through for him again. He picked up the basket and blanket, and stepped out on to the porch. Taking his beloved's hand once more, he led her back around to the steps and toward a flat spot in the clearing, near the edge of the woods. When he had the blanket set to his satisfaction, Darcy helped Elizabeth to sit, and joined her there.

"Ohhh," Elizabeth exclaimed, "Scones!" She almost reverently placed the platter on the blanket. Taking a small crock out of the basket, she pulled the lid off. "Clotted cream! Tell me there is jam in there, as well!"

"Indeed, there is." Darcy pulled out another small crock, then a bowl of sausages, and two cups. Lastly, he pulled the bottle of wine out and began working on the cork.

"Wine, for breakfast?"

The cork popped off just as Elizabeth asked her question. Darcy poured some into one of the cups, handing it to her as he re-
137

plied, "We are celebrating our reunion, are we not? What better to drink in such a case?"

Elizabeth laughed. "Very well, then." She sipped the fragrant liquid. "Mmmm, grape. Excellent. I heartily approve your choice for our celebration." She leaned toward Darcy to accept his kiss.

Darcy and Elizabeth enjoyed their small repast, sharing the events of their time apart, interspersed with kisses. Eventually, they locked themselves inside the folly for a period of more carnal pleasures.

~~~***~~~

When Elizabeth returned to the parsonage, her cousin, William Collins, had already departed for Rosings to discuss his upcoming sermon with his patroness. Collins' wife, Charlotte, was a friend of long-standing to Elizabeth. She looked up from kneading bread in the kitchen at Elizabeth's entrance.

"Good morning, Lizzy! You walked a long time today."

Elizabeth smiled at her friend. "I did. I am sorry; I had not intended to be gone so long, but the sights here are just so beautiful that I got caught up in them." She blushed as she thought of some of the sights she had seen.

Charlotte tilted her head, then opened her mouth and closed it once more. Elizabeth was glad, for that meant she would not have to explain herself further.

"There is a plate beside the stove for you." Charlotte tipped her head toward the Franklin stove along the wall. "Mr. Collins did not wish to wait the meal. He was upset that you did not eat with us, but I was able to persuade him that you were well and would return when you were ready. He wondered if he should not call for a search of the area."

Elizabeth's cheeks darkened. "I was well, and I am sorry to be the cause of concern. I will watch the time more carefully in the future." She took the proffered plate to the table and began to eat. She watched as her friend finished the kneading, then covered the bread with a clean towel and set it beside the warm stove to rise. Then Charlotte wiped off her hands, poured herself a cup of coffee from the pot on the back of the stove, and joined Elizabeth at the table.

"All is well. Mr. Collins must learn that his ways are not everyone's ways. Not that I will tell him that, of course."

Elizabeth smirked. "No, I do not suppose you will. I can only imagine what his response might be. He might fall to the ground, dead and clutching at his chest."

Though Charlotte rolled her eyes, she did not respond. She merely lifted her cup and took a sip.

The ladies were silent as Elizabeth took another bite, chewed, and swallowed. "What is next? I am certain you have a busy day planned." Elizabeth's eyes were on the plate as she scooped up the last morsels of food and put them in her mouth.

Charlotte put her cup down, keeping her fingers looped through the handle. Her left arm was folded across the edge of the table, her hand resting across the inside of the elbow of the arm holding the cup. "I need to walk into the village and do some shopping. I will visit two or three widows while I am there. Would you enjoy coming with me?"

"I would. When do you plan to leave? Have I time to change my gown?"

Charlotte glanced at the clock on the mantel above the kitchen's fireplace. "I would like to go in a quarter-hour. Can you be ready by then?"

Elizabeth stood, sipping the last of her beverage as she did so. "Indeed, I can. I will be right back." With those words, she hurried up the stairs to change.

~~~***~~~

The next afternoon, the parsonage residents received an invitation to attend a dinner at Rosings. Mr. Collins was beside himself at the news.

"Such honor we are shown," Collins exclaimed for the fifth time in as many minutes. "The servant said Lady Catherine's nephew is currently in residence. I did not expect her to have us while he was here." He turned to Elizabeth. "I am certain the addition of such a distinguished personage will add to the awe you already feel about Rosings, Cousin. Though I urge you to restrain your natural tendency to liveliness, I would not wish for you to be so overwhelmed as to be timid."

Elizabeth forced her mien into a sober and stoic expression. It was a struggle to keep her eyes from rolling. *When was I ever in awe of either Rosings or its residents?* she wondered. *He must be mistaking me for his sister-in-law.* When she replied to Collins, she limited her response to, "Thank you."

A few hours later, Collins hurried his wife and guest up the walk toward the great house. This was no great hardship for Elizabeth, for she was eager to see Darcy again, though they had had another rendezvous at the folly just that morning. She did her best to restrain her eagerness. It would not do to display her feelings, lest someone make a connection between her and Darcy. Still, she stepped lively, eager to be in his presence.

They were soon admitted to the house and announced by the butler. As she stood behind her cousin and friend, Elizabeth took a deep breath, holding her hand to her stomach

141

in an effort to calm the butterflies that seemed to have taken up residence there. *I must not seem too eager,* she told herself.

Entering the room, she smiled at the butler. He could not hold her attention for longer than a second or two, however, for at the other end of the chamber, she could see her secret husband. Her heart leapt.

Darcy stood beside and a little behind his aunt's chair. Elizabeth could see that he wore the mask that always covered his face in social situations. Upon closer inspection, though, she could see his eyes scanning her form, and she was glad she had taken extra care with her appearance this evening. Blushing at his perusal, she looked away. Her attention was then claimed by Lady Catherine, who greeted them with an introduction to Darcy.

By previous agreement, Elizabeth and Darcy behaved as though they had never met before. Elizabeth had thought the idea a trifle ridiculous, given their distance from his mother and the lack of communication between Ladies Anne and Catherine, but had been persuaded to her husband's way of thinking through his clever use of mind-blowing kisses and stubborn insistence. In the end, Elizabeth could deny Darcy nothing. If it brought him comfort for them to behave as strangers, she could and would do so.

"Darcy, this is my rector, Mr. Collins, and his wife. Accompanying them is Mr. Collins' cousin, Miss Elizabeth Bennet of Longbourn in Hertfordshire." Lady Catherine waved her hand over the group, then turned to her guests to complete the introductions. "This is my nephew, Mr. Darcy, of Pemberley in Derbyshire, and London."

"How do you do," was echoed by the trio as they performed their bow and curtseys."

Darcy returned their greetings. "I am pleased to make your acquaintance." He opened his mouth to say more, but Lady Catherine beat him to it.

"Sit down, all of you. Our meal will be delayed slightly."

"I hope nothing is amiss," said Collins from the edge of his chair, where he had perched himself.

Lady Catherine waved away his concern. "Nothing that cannot be fixed." She turned to Darcy, who still maintained his position at her side. "Do sit, Nephew. You are far too tall to be standing about when the rest of us are seated."

Darcy gave a sharp nod to his aunt and moved to obey. Elizabeth was seated in a chair at the far end of the seating area, with the Collinses taking up the settee between her and Lady Catherine. The only place left was one beside Anne. Shrugging internally, Darcy stepped across the small space and seated himself beside his cousin. *It is for the best,* he thought. *This way I cannot see Elizabeth without turning toward her and being rude to the rest of the company. I will not be caught staring at her, sitting here.*

"My nephew arrived only yesterday," Lady Catherine announced. "We are always happy when he visits."

"Do you come to Rosings often?" Charlotte had not seen him before, but then, she and Collins had only married six months ago. She was curious about the gentleman, wishing to see if his aunt's praises were given out of blind devotion or truth.

"I usually come but once a year, in the spring, to assist Lady Catherine in the running of her estate. This trip is an exception; her steward has a problem, and she has asked me to come out and look into it." Darcy kept his mask firmly in place and held his body stiffly. He feared that if he allowed himself to relax, he would do something untoward and give away his secret. He could, however, smell Elizabeth's perfume, and in his mind's eye could see her face and form. He wanted nothing more than to sweep her into his arms and kiss her senseless. He clasped his hands tightly in his lap.

Chapter 14

Darcy was saved from more conversation when the bell rang for dinner. He escorted his aunt into the dining room, followed by Anne and Collins, then Charlotte and Elizabeth. As he stood before the table, he watched his wife as the footmen seated the ladies, admiring her gracefulness. Once the chairs of the women had been pushed in, the gentlemen sat. Darcy was pleased that, though he was seated to his aunt's right, Mrs. Collins was on his other side and he could see Elizabeth as she sat across from him and down one place, beside the rector. He was guaranteed good conversation and a sight that was very pleasing to the eye.

Dinner proceeded as all at Rosings did: with Lady Catherine dominating the conversation. This time, she added an interrogation of Elizabeth to the mix, much to the chagrin of half the party.

"Miss Bennet, tell us again about your father's estate. Darcy has not heard about it." Lady Catherine turned to Darcy. "Five daughters and not a son to be found. The estate is entailed to Mr. Collins."

Elizabeth swallowed her mouthful of soup and looked down the table in time to see

Darcy nod once to acknowledge his aunt's words. "Longbourn is a small estate near a market town called Meryton. It has been in our family since the time of William the Conqueror."

Darcy smiled. "The Darcys received Pemberley at about the same time. One of my ancestors did a service for King William and received the plot of land where Pemberley House sits as a reward."

Elizabeth returned Darcy's smile with one of her own. "I believe that is the case for my ancestor, as well. In later generations, additional property was added."

Collins felt it incumbent upon himself to interject his opinion into the conversation at this point. "My father told me many times how prosperous Longbourn was before the current master inherited. When I take his place, which I hope is not soon," Collins hurriedly assured his cousin, "I plan to restore the estate to its former glory."

Elizabeth's temperature rose. She opened her mouth to rebuke her cousin for his intemperate and rude words when Darcy spoke.

"There may have been reasons for Mr. Bennet's lack of success. As the master of my own estate, I can tell you that there are a variety of events that can cause even Pemberley to have several bad seasons and lose income. In my father's time, there was a period of more than ten years where the land did not produce as it should. Every year, either insects, disease, or bad weather killed the crops, and my parents were forced to retrench for a time."

Mr. Collins was struck dumb for a moment to be addressed so by the very wealthy nephew of his most esteemed patroness, to the delight of his fellow diners. The feeling soon passed, however, and within minutes he was alternately praising Darcy and asking for forgiveness for his presumption.

Lady Catherine soon put an end to Collins' obsequious meanderings with another question put to Elizabeth. "Did you tell me, Miss Bennet, that you did not have a governess? Did you say why that was?"

Elizabeth rested her utensils beside her plate. "I did tell you that, yes. We did not have a governess because my father felt none was needed. My mother is a talented manager and runs her household well. She has been able to teach us girls everything we need to know about being the wives of gentlemen. As for other things, like reading, mathematics, and history and the like, my father hired masters for whatever subjects we wished to study. Some of us took full advantage of that offer, and others did not. However, I am certain there can be no good to come of forcing a child to learn subjects that do not interest him, or her for that matter."

Elizabeth's words incited a debate on the merits of education at home versus education at school, a debate that soon turned toward the value of any education at all for girls. She was heartened to hear Darcy supporting her opinions, even when his aunt disagreed.

"I can see no need for girl children to learn anything more than is needed to run a household. Basic reading and sums ought to be enough. Sewing and other needlework, of course, especially for those of the lower classes. Perhaps riding or music lessons. But history and science?" Lady Catherine stuck her nose up in the air, demonstrating her disdain. "Totally unnecessary. Look at my daughter." She gestured to Anne. "She has had no need of lessons at all. Her every need is taken care of, and always will be."

At that point, the mistress of Rosings stood, effectively ending the conversation. The gentlemen rose along with her. "I see no need for a separation of the sexes this evening. Darcy, Collins, the two of you will accompany us to the drawing room. I will have Winters bring the port to us there." Lady Catherine stepped away from the table and waited for her nephew to offer his arm, which she took. The pair of them led the way from the dining room back to the drawing room.

When the Hunsford party returned home later that evening, Darcy was confident that he and Elizabeth had hidden their relationship well. Apparently, not well enough, though, because the door had no more than shut behind them when his aunt began denigrating Elizabeth. Darcy let her go on for a brief time, but quickly grew tired of it.

"Enough, Aunt. If you do not enjoy Miss Bennet's company, you should not invite her here." Darcy's tone was sharp.

"I did not say I do not enjoy her company. I do. However, *you* enjoyed it far too much. Do not think I did not notice you looking at her." Lady Catherine's finger shook at Darcy to punctuate her words.

"It would have been rude to ignore her. I was raised better than that, as were you." Darcy stood and placed his clenched fists on his hips. "I treated Miss Bennet no differently than I did Mrs. Collins or Anne ... or you, for that matter. I am uncertain what you are implying, but whatever it is, I tell you now that I will not be manipulated. It is clear that you are my mother's sister. I will tell you what I have told her: I am master of my estate and am my own man. I will do as I will. I will speak to whomever I wish, whenever I wish. I will come and go as I please. And, I will marry whomever *I* choose without regard to anyone else's desires." Darcy's fists had descended to hang at his sides as his facial features grew sharper and his mien more forbidding. "Do not forget that. Good night, Lady Catherine."

He turned on his heel then and stalked out of the room and up the stairs.

Darcy did not stop until he was in his chambers. He shut the door behind him and walked toward his dressing room, untying his cravat as he moved. "I must be more careful," he muttered. "Though I would not put it past my aunt to see what she wanted to see rather than what was actually there." Stripping off the rest of his clothes and pulling on the nightshirt and robe Smith had laid out for him, Darcy poured a glass of port from the decanter on the dresser and sat in front of the fire. He sipped his drink and thought of Elizabeth until his eyes grew heavy. Then, he crawled into bed and fell into dreams of small children with her fine eyes and ready laugh.

The next morning, Elizabeth returned from her time with Darcy in plenty of time to break her fast with her cousin and his wife. It was a perpetual struggle for Elizabeth to refrain from sarcasm when she spoke to Mr. Collins, and today was no exception. If anything, it was worse.

"My dear cousin, I must warn you most strenuously about flirting with gentlemen, especially those as far above you in consequence as Mr. Darcy."

Elizabeth stopped mid-reach, her hand hovering over the plate of bacon as her head spun toward Collins. Her jaw dropped, and no words would form in her mind. For a full minute, she heard her cousin ramble on about a woman's virtue and throwing her most valuable possession away, but none of it made sense. Finally, she lowered her hand and closed her mouth. "I am sorry, Mr. Collins. I have not the pleasure of understanding you." She glanced at Charlotte, who was looking at her with a sympathetic smile, but quickly turned her attention back to her cousin.

"I was referring to your blatant attempts at making yourself the focus of Mr. Darcy's attentions last night." Collins set his utensil-filled hands down beside his plate as he spoke. "It is unseemly at the least, and probably highly offensive to Lady Catherine. I have no doubt that she will call me to Rosings and have something to say about it."

"Then she will be as batty as you." Elizabeth was incensed, and it came out in her angry choice of words. "I looked no more at Mr. Darcy than I did at anyone else." She stood and threw her napkin on the table in disgust. "If this is what you think of me, perhaps I should curtail my visit. I will send an express to my uncle in London and ask him to come get me."

Charlotte stood, reaching a hand out to Elizabeth. "Please do not go." She turned to her husband, giving him a wide-eyed look that narrowed when he turned his nose up. Speaking to Elizabeth once more, she added, "I am certain Mr. Collins did not mean his words as they sounded."

"Oh, I am quite certain he did," Elizabeth declared. "He has displayed nothing to me but sour grapes since I arrived, going on and on about how any woman would be glad to have such a house, and right in front of you, Charlotte!"

"Lizzy, please." Charlotte pleaded with her friend. She turned to her husband. "I think perhaps we should finish this discussion at another time?"

Collins opened his mouth to speak once more, but something in Charlotte's expression must have caught his attention, because he shut it again. When he did speak, it was to agree with his wife. "I believe you are correct, my dear. We must treat our guest with all due courtesy, and she is clearly distressed." He rose and bowed. "I must make some visits this morning. I will return in time for tea." He took Charlotte's hand and kissed it, then bowed again to Elizabeth before scurrying out the door.

The ladies were quiet for a few minutes once he was gone, but then both sank down into their chairs with a sigh. Elizabeth spoke first.

"I am sorry, Charlotte. I should not have allowed my temper to get the best of me."

"All is well." Charlotte's lips lifted in a soft smile. "Mr. Collins was wrong in what he said to you. I would have been upset, as well, were I you." She paused, looked down and bit her lip, then looked back up and continued, "He suspects an attachment may be forming between you and Mr. Darcy. He told me last night that he noticed the two of you sneaking looks at each other. I told him he is wrong, and that the two of you just met." Charlotte sighed. "I will work on him to remain silent on the topic. I have learned a few things in the last half-year about how to persuade my husband to my way of thinking."

Elizabeth's brows rose and a smirk began to lift the corner of her lips. She managed to keep her comments to, "Indeed." She chose not to address the issue of an attachment between herself and Darcy. The truth would come out soon enough. It was better not to make things more difficult than they already were.

Chapter 15

The next morning, Elizabeth was late for her morning walk with Darcy. She arrived out of breath and red in the face, and clearly aggravated. After a deep kiss, Darcy inquired after her mood.

"Mr. Collins followed me out of the house this morning. It took me forever to lose him; I feared you would be gone by the time I arrived. Charlotte told me yesterday that my cousin thinks we have formed an attachment. He berated me yesterday morning for throwing myself at you at dinner the other night."

"If he followed you this morning, he must believe more than just what he has said. Come." Darcy hurried Elizabeth into the woods, to a small grotto they had found the day before. Formed by the intertwining of the branches of several trees, little sunlight reached the place. There was grass, but it was thin and pale, unlike the thick, dark green lawn around the folly and gardens. It was a perfect place for the couple to settle in for a snuggle and conversation.

It was difficult to get into the glade. There was a deer trail, but thorny bushes grew over into the path in spots, grabbing their clothes and pulling at them. Darcy and

Zoe Burton

Elizabeth had been delighted to find the clearing, because it was so very private.

"We must have a discussion," Darcy began once he and Elizabeth were ensconced in the grotto and seated in a patch of sunlight.

"Yes, I agree." Elizabeth acceded. She snuggled deeper into Darcy's arms. "Have you concluded the business you had with your aunt's steward?"

Darcy wrapped his arms tighter around his wife. "I have. There are one or two things he wishes me to look at before I leave, but that should not take more than one afternoon." He kissed Elizabeth's head where it nestled on his shoulder.

"By tomorrow, you will be free of all duty to Lady Catherine, then." Elizabeth kissed Darcy's chin.

"I will, at least until next Easter. I had hoped to extend my visit, though, to see you. We have not discussed where we are going from here, and now we have the threat of Collins to deal with."

"Were you able to speak with your uncle about Lady Anne?" Elizabeth tensed at the thought of her mother-in-law.

Darcy began to rub one of Elizabeth's arms with his hand. "I was not. I did speak to Richard one evening, and he promised to bring it up to his father when the earl returns from his trip."

"I did not know lords left London when Parliament was in session."

"Generally, they do not. However, one of his colleagues in the House passed away. Uncle attended the funeral." Darcy kissed Elizabeth's forehead. "He should have returned by the time I get back to London, even if I do as I think I should and leave early."

Elizabeth merely nodded, too afraid she would cry if she tried to speak. She hated being apart from Darcy and looked forward to the day they could remain together forever, openly married.

"Do not cry, my love. I know you want to. I grieve at the thought of leaving you behind again as much as you do. I need to deal with my mother before we can announce our news to the world. I need to keep you safe from her machinations." Darcy lifted her chin and continued, "Do you understand?" He kissed Elizabeth's upturned lips, softly at first but then more deeply. Tearing himself away, he stroked her cheek with his thumb. "Tell me you understand."

"I do," Elizabeth whispered. "I dread the separation, but I do understand the need for it. It is just that I feel safer with you near."

Darcy kissed his wife again. "I know. I plan to hire guards for you. Richard gave me the names of a few former soldiers in this area who were trained for covert missions. They have been retired from service to the Crown due to injuries, but my cousin assures me that they are capable of protecting anyone. They will only be able to guard you if you are away from Rosings, mind. I cannot hire them to protect you here without a danger of our secret being exposed; but if you leave Rosings or the parsonage, they will be following you."

Elizabeth nodded, her cheek rubbing over his waistcoat and shirt. "I understand. Did you tell your cousin about us?"

"No. I dared not. I trust him to keep my secrets, as a rule, but this is too important. He might feel it necessary to ride to the rescue and thwart all our plans without meaning to."

Elizabeth chuckled. "I see." She then fell silent as she considered all they had spoken about. Finally, she asked, "When do you plan to leave?"

"Tomorrow, I think. My aunt will know that my business is done. To stay longer would invite more suspicion than we already have."

Gripping Darcy's waist tighter, Elizabeth lifted her face. "Then, let us make the most of this last morning together. How long will our separation be, this time?"

Darcy brushed his lips over Elizabeth's before he answered. "Hopefully not more than another fortnight. Just until my mother has been dealt with. I promise." Darcy's whispered words were followed by a passionate kiss, and he and Elizabeth spent what remained of their final morning together at Rosings in the glade, making love.

Darcy House, London

Lady Anne Darcy accepted the mail from the butler, Mr. Baxter, and strolled into her study to go through it. She opened letter after letter, most of them invitations to balls and soirees held by her peers. One was from her late husband's sister, one from her own sister, and two were from Scotland. She tossed Lady Catherine's note to the side. She was not going to be in a mood for dealing with her sibling for a while yet. Though impatient to read the two, Lady Anne forced herself to peruse the missive from Mrs. Emma Darcy first. Finding it full of nothing but news about Emma's new grandchild, Lady Anne tossed it on the desk and turned her attention to the missives she truly wanted to read.

Choosing to peruse a more lighthearted missive before reading the more important one, the first letter Lady Anne opened was from Elspeth Brodie. Similar to the one from Emma Darcy, it was full of news of her children and a very nice expression of delight at Lady Anne's recent visit. Lady Anne smiled. Even though Elspeth was below her in station, Lady Anne did like the other woman.

Next, Lady Anne picked up the last letter, a note from an investigator in Dumfries.

Lady Anne had hired the man via one of her most loyal servants, and tasked the agent with discovering where her son had married, and if he had. She had been specific when she noted that it did not matter to her how the investigator found the information, just that she wanted it. She had paid a princely sum for his services, as well. She expected good information from him, and now she was about to find out if he was worth the expense.

Eagerly, Lady Anne broke the seal of the letter and unfolded it. She read quickly at first, as the top portion of the note listed the places the man had looked in the beginning of his investigation. Suddenly, she stopped and began reading more carefully.

> *I should have started looking in Gretna Green, for that is where I found the information you seek. The clergyman there would not reveal any information and refused to allow me to see the register, but of course, that did not stop me. Once I asked around a bit and heard rumors of a large donation, I was certain I would find what I sought. Sure enough, when I broke into the church that night and searched the register, there were the names I was looking for: Fitzwilliam Darcy and Elizabeth Bennet. I took the time to make a copy of the page and have enclosed it within this missive. I*

expect final payment for my services within a fortnight.

Lady Anne reread the paragraph, anger and elation rising together in her breast. Her pulse began to pound. She leapt from her seat, letter in her hand, and began pacing the width of the room. Her skirts swished as she turned at each end of the chamber. She muttered to herself as she considered her next steps.

"She definitely needs to die now. Fitzwilliam will have a year or two of mourning, but then I will present the best of the heiresses that year, and he will have to select one.

"Now, how to accomplish this? Where is the little chit? How will I discover her current location?" Lady Anne marched back and forth several more times as she considered and discarded several options. Then, she remembered that her sister had written to her. "Catherine will know how best to advise me. I will read her letter now, and in my reply, will ask her for assistance." So saying, Lady Anne took up the missive from Kent and broke open the seal, dropping onto a settee in front of the fire and starting to read.

"So," Lady Anne exclaimed a few minutes later. "Elizabeth Bennet is in Kent, visiting Catherine's rector and his wife. That works out very well for me." She read a little further. "Fitzwilliam reports he is almost finished with the work he was doing for her. She

161

thinks he will be leaving her on Monday. Very well." She lowered the letter to her lap, retaining it in her grasp. Her eyes darted back and forth as she made a list in her mind of what she would do. When she had settled it, she rose to her feet and sat herself again at her desk. Composing a quick note, she rang for a servant to post it. Then, she readied herself for a planned outing—a night at the theatre with two of her friends.

The next day, Lady Anne ascended into her carriage, instructing the coachman to drive her to Bow Street. Though he looked at her with wide eyes, the driver did not say anything to her. Soon, Lady Anne was descending out of the carriage, handed out by a groom.

"Come with me," Lady Anne instructed the servant. Turning on her heel, she strode along the street almost to the corner of Russell Street, where stood a tea shop right beside a coffee shop. Lady Anne entered the tea shop, instructing the groom to go to the counter and order her a pot of tea and a scone. As she waited for it to be served, she observed the street outside the window. Her tea and pastry were brought to her just as a gentleman entered alone, searching the room with his gaze. Lady Anne gestured to the groom to move closer and stand behind her and then waited for the stranger to approach.

"Would you be the lady looking to hire someone?" The man's voice was gruff. He was dressed well, though of a lower quality than the gentlemen of Lady Anne's acquaintance.

"I am. You may be seated." She gestured to the chair opposite her at the small table. "Would you care for tea?"

The man, called John Markham by those who needed to know such details, sat but declined Lady Anne's offer of refreshment. "No, thank you, Madam. I understand you require some work to be done."

"Indeed, I do. I was given your name long ago by a trusted … friend. I was told you are able to permanently solve problems of all kinds." Lady Anne lifted her cup to take a sip of tea, her eyes watchful over the rim.

"I generally am capable of that. What kind of problem are you looking to have solved?"

Lady Anne leaned forward, her intense gaze looking Markham in the eyes. She pitched her voice low, keeping her words between her and her tablemate. "There is a fortune hunter who has gotten her claws in my son. I want her dead."

Markham did not blink an eye. He had been around enough to know that ladies of the gentry were just as bloodthirsty as the lowest murderer in Seven Dials. "Where is this woman to be found?"

Lady Anne leaned back in her chair. "Kent. She is staying with my sister's rector and his wife in the parsonage at Hunsford."

"Kent is half a day's ride. It will cost you extra."

"I will pay whatever is required. If the situation were different, I would take care of the chit myself."

"Very well, then." Markham thought a minute, laying a plan out in his mind. "The deed must be carried out in a way that does not lead back to me, which means it will not lead to you, either. I will require a horse and carriage and more men. We will abduct the girl and take her elsewhere to perform the act."

"I care not how you handle it." Lady Anne rose, dropping a small bag of coins onto the table. "Just see that it is done. I expect regular reports, and proof that you have completed the task."

Markham stood, tugging on his cap before scooping up the bag and depositing the heavy item in his pocket. "As you wish."

Chapter 16

Michael Larksworth shut the door to Lady Anne's carriage and climbed up to sit beside the coachman. Though generally an amiable man, what the groom had heard in the tea shop had shaken him, and he spent the entire ride back to Darcy House thinking about it.

Hours later, after the horses had been cooled, fed, and groomed and the carriage put away, Larksworth gathered with the rest of the staff in the kitchen of the townhouse for a meal. He accepted his plate with thanks and dug in, his mind still turning over the events of the morning. The other servants began to notice his changed behaviour, but Larksworth did not wish to speak of it, and so shrugged off their concerns.

When he pushed away from the table, thanking the cook for the meal, the combination coachman and stablemaster, a heavy man of medium height and indefinable age named Harold Grey, stood with him. They walked back to the stables together, and as they entered, Harold spoke.

"I've noticed you've been far quieter than you're usual habit today."

Larksworth lowered his chin to his chest and inhaled through his nose. Harold Grey was a kindly man, and reminded Larksworth of his own father. Grey had the reputation of being honest and reliable. Larksworth lifted his head and, seeing the concern and kindness in his supervisor's mien, decided that if anyone could help him understand what he heard and what to do about it, Harold Grey was the man. "I've something on my mind that I know not what to do with."

"Would you like to talk about it?" Grey gestured with his hand to his small office in the back of the compact stable.

Larksworth nodded, then followed Grey into the room.

Grey looked about to make sure no one was hanging around, and then shut the door. Sitting down behind his desk, he gestured to another small chair. "Have a seat." He leaned back and rested his hands on his midsection, fingers linked together. "Tell me what has happened. Something in that shop with the mistress?"

Larksworth nodded, noting the sharp interest in Grey's eyes. "I could swear I heard her order the death of another woman." The footman saw that he had Grey's full attention when the other man suddenly went very still. Larksworth then related everything that happened in the shop from the moment he and Lady Anne entered until they left.

Grey remained quiet until the groom finished speaking. "You're for certain that's what you heard? You said she was speaking quietly."

"Aye, she was, but I have excellent hearing. I know what I heard. I'll stand by that if you pull my fingernails out, one at a time."

Grey's brows lifted at Larksworth's words, but he chuckled. "No one's going to do that. If you say you heard it, then you did. Are you worried about what to do?"

"I am. I enjoy my position here, and I'd not wish to be sacked for crossing the mistress. Besides, from what I heard today, I could very well end up dead for it. I like my life even better than I do my employment. Still, it's not right to order someone else's murder. It's ... cold-blooded." He shivered. "I never imagined something so evil coming out of a lady so fine."

"Of course." Grey thought for a bit, looking at his desk instead of his companion. Finally, he looked up. "Do not worry a minute more about this. I know what needs to be done and I'll take care of it." He held up a hand when Larksworth began to protest. "I'll not be calling the magistrate or the runners, I promise. You just go on and finish your chores and turn in. Do not speak of what you heard to anyone. As a matter of fact, don't tell anyone about this conversation, either. Understand?"

"Yes, sir," Larksworth nodded, relieved to have the issue off his conscience and more than happy to leave it in Grey's capable hands. He stood when the coachman told him to go, pulling on his cap and hastening away.

Grey waited for a half-hour in his office, then got up and strolled out of the stable. He made his way down the alley behind the row of great houses to the corner, then turned left down that alley. At the next intersection, he made another left-hand turn, coming out on the other side of Grosvenor Square from Darcy House. He knocked on the door to the servant's entrance of a townhouse there, and was swiftly admitted. Within a few minutes, he was being shown into the master's study.

"Grey, good to see you." Lord Matlock shook the coachman's hand and gestured for him to sit down. "If you are here, you must have some news about my sister."

"I do, your lordship."

"Well, spit it out, then. I have a feeling I already know, based on a letter from my nephew and a note from my son." Matlock gestured to papers that lay on his desk. "Not home a quarter hour and I am bombarded with bad news." He shook his head.

Grey relayed everything Larksworth had told him, leaving out no detail. He included in his retelling the state of mind the groom had been in from the time he had followed Lady Anne out of the tea shop until he left Grey's office. "It disturbed him greatly. I reassured him I knew what to do and that he was not to worry further, but I would imagine he'll avoid her as much as he can."

Matlock sighed. "Yes, I would imagine the same." He stood. "Thank you again, Grey. You have once more served me well. The best money I ever spent was hiring you to watch Darcy House and my sister." Reaching in his desk, Matlock took out some coins and pressed them into Grey's hand. "I will take it from here."

Grey accepted the coins, thanked Lord Matlock, and tugged on his cap. Then, he left the study and was gone.

~~~***~~~

Darcy arrived home from Kent at midday on Saturday. Entering the house, he handed his hat, gloves, and walking stick to Mr. Baxter and listened as the butler gave him a quick update about what had happened in his absence. With a nod, Darcy dismissed the man and strode through the entry hall and into his study.

Darcy always stopped and inhaled when he entered this room. He did the same at Pemberley. Both chambers were decorated the same way, in dark paneling and heavy wooden furniture. The scent of beeswax with an underlying hint of cigar smoke teased his nos-

169

trils. Darcy missed his father most when he entered the study at either house. Both rooms had been the center of power when the elder Darcy was alive, and the masculine sights and smells brought happy memories of his father to Darcy's mind.

Letting out his breath and stepping further into the room, Darcy relaxed a bit. Spotting the pile of correspondence that Baxter had told him about on the desk, Darcy picked it up and dropped into his chair to begin the task of sorting the mail into piles. Reaching one that bore the handwriting and seal of the Earl of Matlock, he stopped, dropping the remaining letters haphazardly on top of the others and breaking open the one from his uncle.

July 28, 1810

Darcy,

I am in receipt of your most recent missive and have read Richard's, as well. Attend me as soon as you arrive in town. It is a matter of vital importance. Do not tell your mother you are coming.

Matlock

Darcy dropped the note on the desk and began to walk away. Thinking better of it, he stopped suddenly, turning around to pick the letter up again, fold it, and tuck it into the pocket of his coat. Then, he went back out into the hall and called for Mr. Baxter.

"Where is Mrs. Darcy?" he asked.

"She is from home, sir. I believe she said she was making calls today."

"Excellent. Call for a horse to be saddled for me and brought around to the service entrance. I will need my hat and gloves. Do not tell my mother that I have arrived, unless she notices and says something to you. If she does, tell her I went out immediately and did not tell you where I was going."

"Very good, sir." Baxter bowed slightly.

Darcy lowered his voice. "If I am needed, and I mean truly needed, send word to Matlock House. They will know how to find me."

"Yes, sir." Baxter handed the gloves and top hat to his master and set about ordering the horse before following Darcy to the kitchen.

Darcy waited in the mews behind the house for his ride to be brought out from the stable. Tugging on his gloves, when the groom approached leading the animal, he thanked the lad, flipping him a coin. Then, he mounted and nudged the gelding into a walk. Taking the same route his coachman had the day before, Darcy arrived at his uncle's back door within minutes. There, he handed the reins to a servant, asking the boy to tie the horse inside the stable and out of sight. Assured that his mount would not be seen from the street, Darcy entered through the kitchen door. Soon, he was escorted into his uncle's library.

"Darcy," Lord Matlock rose as he greeted his nephew. "Good to see you. I had not anticipated your attendance for another day or two."

"I left Rosings earlier than I planned to." Darcy bowed to his uncle. "I take it you received my note?"

Matlock nodded as he gestured to Darcy to take a seat before the fire. "Yours as well as Richard's. I have other, related, news, as well, but I think it best that you tell me what you found, first."

Darcy accepted the glass of port his uncle offered and sipped it while his mother's brother poured a glass of his own and settled into the chair beside him. Then, he began. "Mother arrived in Scotland two weeks after I did, uninvited and completely unexpected. You recall that I made that visit to check on the state of affairs at Glenmoor?" He cocked his brow at his uncle and, receiving the elder gentleman's assurance that he did remember, Darcy continued. "She had no more than removed her hat before she began an argument with me." Darcy then recounted the entire week-long visit before describing the journal he had found. "You know as well as I that Mother is temperamental, but this shocked me to my core."

"Did you think to bring the diary with you?"

"No, I admit I did not. I replaced it where I found it because I did not wish to incite her ire. Tell me," Darcy pleaded with his uncle. "My father ... he did not die because his horse threw him, did he?"

Matlock sighed. He had avoided this conversation for years, for the simple reason that he had only suspicions about his brother's death. "He did die after the accident, but I do believe he would have survived had something else not been happening. I did not realize until the laying out, because I had not seen your father in nearly a year, but his skin was very white. The servants at Pemberley told me of odd behavior and illnesses on his part." He shrugged. "I knew something was not right, but had nothing to base any assumptions on.

"Your mother was not about to tell me the truth. She was a bully when we were children. I do not know that I have ever told you of that, though I did mention it to your father once, right before their wedding. There was nothing he could do about it, of course. The marriage was arranged, and the ceremony was scheduled for the next day.

"George took a strong hand with your mother from the first moment of his marriage, and he told me it was because of my words to him that he did so. We gave that same advice to you, if you recall."

"You did, and I have." Darcy looked down at his hands, which held his drink. He swirled the glass and watched the motion of the port as it sloshed around. He began speaking, looking up as he did so. "So, Father was sick before he died. One of the entries in Mother's journal mentions his death. Not in so many words, but the date matches, and in the entry, she admits to harming him." He paused again, his features twisted as grief overtook him. "What is wrong with her?"

Chapter 17

Matlock sighed and stared at his own empty glass. "I do not know, Son. Sometimes, there is no way to explain why people are the way they are. Anne was raised no differently than Catherine or me. She was the youngest and perhaps a bit spoiled, and certainly, my sisters were both raised with the expectation that their status as the daughters of an earl would grant them whatever they wished. Perhaps that is the problem. Catherine is no saint, either, though I have never heard anything about her that leads me to think her anything other than interfering and controlling."

Darcy was silent as he worked to regain control of his emotions. He stared into the fire until he was able to speak calmly. "I sense there is more than what you have told me."

"Yes. I have a man installed in your household to watch and listen for my sister's antics." Matlock glanced at Darcy, whose brows had risen in question. "Harold Grey."

"My coachman," Darcy murmured. "I have long wondered about him. He has sharp eyes and has always seemed to prefer serving Mother more than me."

Matlock chuckled. "It is not that he prefers her, it is that he was hired to keep an eye on her." He pointed at Darcy when the younger man smiled. "I, for one, am grateful I had the foresight to convince your mother to hire him. The previous man wanted to retire after your father's death; that gave me the perfect opening. With George gone, Anne had no one to press her to behave rationally. Grey has proved invaluable more than once."

"What has he told you now?"

"Brace yourself," Matlock said with a sigh. "One of the grooms accompanied your mother into a tea shop yesterday, where she met a man. The groom swears she paid the man to kill a young lady who she called a fortune hunter. She mentioned that the chit was after you."

Darcy gasped, going pale at his uncle's words.

"What is wrong?" Matlock grabbed Darcy's glass, which he was in danger of shattering in his grip.

"Does this young lady have a name?" Darcy's hands gripped the arms of the chair. He desperately hoped the name that came off his uncle's lips would not be that of his beloved.

"She does. Miss Elizabeth Bennet."

Darcy shot up and out of the chair. "She must be stopped. What has been done?"

Matlock rose with his nephew, alarmed at Darcy's pallor and anguished words. "I have hired runners to find the man she hired. I have impressed upon them the importance of speed in the resolution of the matter, but all we can do is wait."

"What about Mother?"

Matlock sighed. "I do not know. It may be possible to declare her insane, but that will damage the reputations of all of us, Darcy and Fitzwilliam alike. You have a sister to marry off and I have a son. Not to mention that the clout I have in Parliament will be diminished, and there is legislation that I need backing on. Above all that, she will be sent to Bedlam if we do it, and I do not know that I can stomach my baby sister living in those conditions, do you?"

Darcy shook his head. "No, I cannot. I do not want that for her. Despite her actions toward me over the years, I cannot and will not subject her to such degradation. Nor do I wish her to hang, and you know that punishment is meted out no matter the gender or station of the convicted."

"All we really have is our power as gentlemen. Your mother has her own fortune, but you control the purse strings. We will have to confront her, but we can offer her a home somewhere. Perhaps in Scotland, though restricting her to the dower house, either at Pemberley or Matlock might suffice. Then, cut off her funds. You will need to hire servants that will not bow to her wishes, and you may be required to pay them handsomely." Matlock clasped Darcy's shoulder. "We will handle this within the family, Darcy. There will be no shame for her or you or any of us."

"The shame is already there, Uncle," Darcy exclaimed bitterly. "Who can proclaim pride in a mother who abuses and kills those below her?" Darcy's sister's face flashed before his eyes. "Georgiana! Has she suffered under our mother's thumb? Thank goodness she is at school so much of the time!"

Matlock hesitated, but could be nothing less than honest. "I do not know how Anne behaves with Georgiana. Like most in our society, my sister keeps her child in the nursery. When your sister is ready to come out, we will see them interact, but other than a few minutes when we visit, we do not know. I sincerely hope she is not harming Georgiana in any way, but I have no way to know right now."

"I know, truly I do." Darcy paused, taking a deep breath and then using it to puff out his cheeks as he let it out. "I will try to speak to my sister soon. In the meantime," he straightened. "I must return to Kent immediately. I must try to stop this man." He bowed to his surprised uncle and, before the man could gather his wits enough to reply, stalked out of the room and toward the back of the house.

Matlock jumped as his brain caught up with his other senses, and raced after his nephew, catching him halfway through the kitchen. "Darcy!" he called. "Darcy!" Finally reaching him, the earl grabbed Darcy's arm, stopping him in his tracks. "Wait!" Panting at the exertion, he ignored the hard stare that drilled into him, and waved at the door. "You cannot leave tonight. It is nearly dark, and you know as well as I that the roads outside of the city are dangerous. You will not arrive in Kent until very early in the morning, and can do nothing until day breaks, anyway. Please, promise me you will wait until morning to leave. At the least, dawn."

The tension that filled Darcy's frame did not leave him as he listened to his uncle. All he knew was that he needed to get to Elizabeth before this unknown criminal did. He stared at the door, the knowledge that his uncle was correct warring with his primal need to protect the wife no one knew he had. The logic of his uncle's argument soon won out, though, and Darcy conceded. After promising to sleep as much as he could tonight, he walked out the door and rode back to Darcy House the way he came.

Upon arriving at his home, Darcy followed the niggling feeling he had in his stomach that he needed to keep Lady Anne from being aware that he was home. He knew she would not pay any mind to his valet, because

Smith kept to the servant's stairs and basement areas of the house when he was not tending to Darcy. Lady Anne rarely entered that level of the home, if ever. Following his intuition, Darcy used the servant's stairs to go up to his suite of rooms. He arrived to find his valet waiting with hot water.

"What have you heard while I was out?" Darcy began to untie his cravat as he spoke.

"Lady Anne is not expecting you for two more days, according to the housekeeper. I asked her to keep your presence quiet for now. She seemed confused, but agreed." Smith accepted the cravat he was handed and watched as his master began shedding his coat.

"Confused?" Darcy unbuttoned his waistcoat.

"Several times in the last few years, she has expressed a desire for you and your mother to become closer. I think it dismays her to see that you remain distant." Smith shrugged when Darcy's right brow rose. "She is a romantic at heart, I suspect. I do not know how she successfully manages a staff of young ladies when she insists on seeing the best in everyone and ignoring the worst."

Darcy rolled his eyes and snorted. "Indeed." He pulled his shirt over his head, handing it to Smith and sitting on the chair so his man could pull his boots off. "Anything else?"

"Nothing unusual. Lady Anne has been out nearly every evening since she got back from Scotland. Her routine is the same as always, though she did move her at-home day from Friday this week to Monday next week. Mrs. Bishop said Mrs. Darcy ordered the carriage, instead, and was gone an hour or so. She does not know where your mother went, and Lady Anne's maid does not speak of her mistress, so no one has asked her." Smith spoke to Darcy's boots as he pulled them off, but he spoke clearly enough that Darcy heard him.

Darcy nodded as he rose to remove his breeches and stockings. "Very well." He took two steps to the ewer and began washing himself. "I will be travelling back to Kent tomorrow at first light, on horseback. I want you to go ahead of me. As early as you will be leaving, you should be able to get away without my mother discovering you." Taking the towel his valet offered him, Darcy began to dry himself. "My wife is in danger; I am only waiting until tomorrow because it will be too late to do anything, find anything, if I arrive in the middle of the night."

Smith handed his master a nightshirt and then bowed. "Very good, Sir. Am I to present myself at Rosings, then?"

Darcy pulled the nightshirt on. "No. Stop at the Rose in Hunsford Village and wait for word. I do not know what I will find; I may need a physician or the magistrate. Hopefully," he sighed, "I will find my Mrs. Darcy hearty and hale, but I do not know."

"Will you be facing this threat alone?" Smith's mien remained impassive, but there was a stiffness to his manner that let Darcy know he was concerned.

"I am going to attempt to contact the guards I hired first and get a report. He and his men cannot enter Rosings, but they will likely see anyone who attempts to approach the parsonage, and if Elizabeth is removed from the property, they are authorized to rescue her." Darcy's shoulders slumped. "That will be all. I am going to try to sleep, though I am certain I will spend the night praying for her safety, instead."

Smith bowed again and watched Darcy leave the dressing room for the bedchamber and close the door behind him. Shaking his head, he sent a prayer of his own up, and then began repacking the items he had only hours ago unpacked.

Chapter 18

Hunsford, Kent, Saturday morning

John Markham rode atop the driver's seat of the small carriage as it approached the village of Hunsford. Beside him was the man he had hired to assist him in his mission, Nicholas Stapleton. Markham had chosen this particular fellow because he knew how to drive, a skill that might be needed, should he have to quickly move the young lady he was hired to kill. Markham himself preferred to walk and did not know how to drive. He was not a man who enjoyed moving very quickly, despite the fact that his chosen profession often required his swift removal from one location to another. He disliked horses and could not tell a bridle from a bit.

Stapleton, on the other hand, had a reputation for enjoying speed and for making an animal move as fast as he could. He had outrun the law both on horseback and in an equipage more times than he could count, though that was not saying much, since he could not count past three. In any case, Stapleton's skill with horses and carriages, added to his willingness to do anything for money, was what got him hired for this job.

The pair of them pulled up in front of the inn on the high street of the town and parked the team. They climbed down and went inside for a pint and a bite to eat, and while there, paid for a room.

As they enjoyed a quick repast, the pair listened to the conversations around them. Markham quickly surmised that his target was still at the parsonage. Further, he learned that she enjoyed walking out. Leaning over to his companion, he spoke quietly. "We need to find this church. The rector's residence, if I understand these things correctly, is near it."

Stapleton nodded, lifting his tankard to his lips and taking a large gulp. "Do ye want to snoop around a bit and get the lay of the land before we do the deed?"

Markham nodded. "I do." He gestured with his head to the group of men at the table beside them, whose conversation they had overheard. "You heard them, didn't you? The young lady visiting the parsonage likes to go for walks. We'll head over there and look around, see what the best way to approach is. With any luck, this information will allow us to complete the mission and return to London before dark tomorrow."

Stapleton finished his ale and set the tankard down hard. "Let's go, then, and see what's what." He rose. "I need to make a call. I'll meet ye out front in a few minutes."

"I'm right behind you." Markham paid the girl for their meals and followed Stapleton to the outhouse behind the inn.

A few minutes later, the two men met in front of the building and began walking the town. They had decided to first walk away from the church as a way to cover their tracks, but soon they were making the stroll to the pair of buildings on the outskirts of the town, just over a half-mile away. As they walked, their sharp eyes took in every detail. They strolled up the dusty road to where a large iron gate indicated the entrance to an estate. They turned right to walk down the lane that separated the clearly prosperous property on one side from the humble parsonage on the other. They continued past the garden and beehives at the back of the rector's home, stopping when they realized that they had entered an orchard that was likely part of the nearby estate. Silently, they indicated their agreement to return the way they came.

Not more than a quarter-hour later, Stapleton spoke. "Did ye see those men, hanging about?"

"I did. I saw one on this side of the church and one across the road from the parsonage. I wonder at their presence. The lady that hired us said nothing about others being sent here, so maybe the one that owns the estate hired them." He shrugged. "Or, someone else could have. Without knowing their purpose, we can't do anything about them."

"There was one in the churchyard, too. I saw him as we walked past the parsonage garden the first time." Stapleton became quiet as he and his companion thought about the implications of three random men hiding in plain sight.

Markham was the first to break the silence this time. "I saw no one on the other side, where that fancy place is. Rosings, I think the lady called it."

Stapleton shook his head. "I didn't, neither, nor in amongst the apple trees behind the beehives. We can approach the house from that side, but we'll have to get past those three gents."

"You're right, we will. I think they were watching the church or the parsonage, which probably means this girl we're here for is worth something to someone. We'll have to think of a way to grab her without going past the church again."

The pair thought some more, but remained silent, going up to the room they were going to share for the night. When they were alone, they took up the conversation again, but quietly so as not to be overheard through the thin walls.

"What about this?" Stapleton asked. "We go east out of town there by the smithy, then turn to tha north. We should find ourselves in that orchard before too long. We can hide amongst the trees in the grove on the estate and wait for tha gel to come out."

Markham stroked his chin as he examined his accomplice's idea from all angles. "We should follow the chit into the woods and grab her there."

"Are we goin' ta kill her on the estate, or take her somewhere?"

"Depends, I guess, on what's going on at the time. If she puts up too much of a fight, we'll do her in on the estate, but I'd rather take her out in a field somewhere. By the time anyone would find the body, you and I would be well on our way to London." Markham reiterated that he had no intention of getting caught. "I've gotten away clean all these years, I don't plan to start rotting in jail now."

"Me, neither," Stapleton fervently declared. "What about the carriage? Are we even gonna use it?"

"I had originally intended to. However, since we have to go through fields to get to the girl, I guess we won't. If she's small enough, she won't be too hard to carry."

Stapleton snorted. "When have ye seen one a them rich ladies be small?"

"Never," Markham admitted, "but then, I've not seen that many fine ladies in my life. Besides, this chit likes to walk. You heard that farmer downstairs. Says she walks for hours. Described her figure as light."

"'Tis true," Stapleton nodded. "Very well, then. We'll carry 'er. What if she fights?"

"Then, we knock her out. It'll make killing her that much easier." Markham didn't enjoy killing, though it didn't repulse him, either. His goal was to do every job quickly and cleanly and get away from the area as fast as possible.

"Verra well. What time do ye want to head out there?"

"Let's wait a bit, then go down and have some drinks. When the innkeeper starts shooing people out, we can follow like we belong with that crowd. It'll be well after dark then, and we'll have to find that orchard with only moonlight to see by, but we can hunker down in the trees and sleep, then be awake at first light in case the girl walks early."

"Good plan. I'm goin' ta sleep a while now. Wake me when ye're ready to go down." Stapleton lay back on the bed, stretching out and getting comfortable. Within moments, he was asleep.

Markham followed suit, laying down on the settee situated before the fireplace.

Darcy House, London

Sunday morning at dawn

Darcy rose from his bed after a sleepless night while the world was still dark. The smallest hint of the sun's rays peeked up above the houses on Grosvenor Square. He thought Smith must have slept in the dressing room, because the valet was ready for the morning, with a set of riding clothes laid out for the master and a pitcher of hot water for washing.

Darcy readied himself swiftly. He debated getting a shave; though Smith was prepared, Darcy was anxious to leave. A glance out the window at the still-dark city convinced him that he had time, so he submitted to the activity.

Finally clean-shaven and ready to go, Darcy reviewed the plan with Smith. "I want you to start out ahead of me. I have already told the coachman to push the horses as much as he can to get you there as quickly as possible. I do not know what I will find, though I prayed all night that Mrs. Darcy would wait to walk out until after church."

"Yes, Sir. I will likely arrive in Hunsford after you do, but I will wait at the Rose for your instructions."

"Yes, good." Darcy paced distractedly while drinking the coffee Smith had brought up.

"I have taken the liberty of packing a saddlebag with food and another with weapons." Smith pulled the items out of the closet and laid them on the bed. "You will certainly

189

need the former and will possibly require the latter."

"Good thinking!" Darcy was more enthused about the contents of the saddlebags than he had been anything else so far this day. "I will see you in a few hours." He dismissed the valet, listening to the man's footsteps as he hastened down the stairs. Darcy looked out the window in time to see the carriage containing his personal servant pull away from the house. He finished his coffee, made use of the chamber pot, and then took up the bags and slung them over his shoulder. By the time the sky was beginning to lighten, he was in the stable, saddling his favorite mount, Apollo.

Darcy headed toward Kent with every muscle in his body tense. He knew he should have eaten, but his stomach threatened to reject even the coffee he had consumed. He felt jumpy and nervous. Once he reached the edge of London, he nudged the horse into a faster gait.

Darcy's mind was full of Elizabeth. Where was she right now? Was she safe in her bed in the parsonage, or was she crying for him in an abandoned building somewhere? Was she sleeping, or lying awake in terror? He prayed anew with each scenario that his fertile imagination conjured up; prayed for Elizabeth's safety and good health, and for her return to his arms. He did not want to think about his life without her.

Darcy urged Apollo to keep going, sometimes at a gallop, sometimes a trot or canter, sometimes a walk. They stopped for nothing more than to allow Darcy to relieve himself once and for Apollo to eat some grass and drink a bit of water, then they were back on the road. They made good time this way, and Darcy arrived at Hunsford well before the church bell began to ring.

Rosings, Kent

The Folly

Elizabeth squinted up at the sun and realized that it was past time for her to be back at the parsonage. Picking up the remains of her breakfast—an apple core and a crust of bread—she wiped her eyes and stood. She had been thinking about Darcy. She missed him greatly and was eager to see him again. One of the biggest drawbacks of their arrangement was that they could not correspond, and though he had only left a day ago, she would have liked a note telling her of his safe arrival.

Tossing the apple core and bread scrap toward the woods, Elizabeth climbed down the few steps of the folly to the familiar path. She kept her head down as she began to walk. She was not in a state where she could appreciate the beauty. She never noticed the unnatural stillness that came over the forest around her.

Chapter 19

Darcy pulled Apollo to a stop in front of the parsonage and prayed as he approached the house that Mrs. Collins or a servant would answer the door instead of Mr. Collins. He knocked and waited. When the door was finally opened, he breathed a sigh of relief.

"Mr. Darcy! Come in, please. My husband is already at the church; did you need to speak to him?" Charlotte's brows had risen when she saw who it was at her door, but she stepped back to allow the gentleman in.

"Thank you, no. I am here on a matter of utmost urgency. Is Miss Bennet still in residence?" Darcy had removed his hat and was gripping it tightly.

Charlotte could see from Darcy's furrowed brow and terse manner of speaking that he was distressed. She wondered why he needed to speak to her friend, but she was not going to question him. Despite her husband's antics and Elizabeth's denials, she thought Mr. Darcy might like her friend. "She has not gone home yet, no, but she is not within at the moment. She went for a walk this morning." Charlotte looked around to peek at the clock on the wall in her husband's parlour, which could be seen from where she stood. "As a matter of fact, she should have been back already. I wonder where she is?" Charlotte turned back to the door to see that Darcy had paled. "Are you well?"

"Did she say where she was walking today?" Darcy was already putting his hat back on his head and backing down the steps.

"She said she had discovered a quiet glade near the folly. I assume that is where she went, but do not know for certain."

"Thank you, Mrs. Collins. You have been most helpful." Darcy sketched a quick bow and untied Apollo, leaping into the saddle and kicking the animal into motion.

Charlotte waved him off, confused and not a little concerned about Elizabeth. *If anyone can find her, Mr. Darcy can. He seems to know the area very well.* With those thoughts, she closed the door and went to sit in the parlour to await her friend.

Darcy took off down the lane and as he did so, he spotted one of the guards he had hired to watch his wife. He pulled Apollo to a stop again, gesturing to the man to come near.

The guard had recognized Darcy when he rode up to the parsonage and noted the gentleman's state of near-panic. When Darcy stopped and gestured him near, he hastened to the horse's side.

"I have learned of a plot to harm the young lady you were hired to protect. She went walking this morning."

"She did," the guard agreed, "but she walked onto Rosings property, so we did not follow."

"I need you to gather your fellows and follow me onto the estate. Leave my aunt to me; I will deal with her later. I require your assistance."

"Yes, Sir!" The ex-soldier jumped back to allow Darcy to spur Apollo into motion once more, then waved in the direction of his companion. The third guard, having seen this, came out from the churchyard where he had been concealed. The three ran into the woods behind Darcy.

Darcy leaned low over Apollo's neck as he sped down the path toward the folly. As he approached, he thought he heard a cry, but it was too faint and the sound of the horse's hooves drowned it out. Finally, he entered the clearing that contained the small building that held so many happy memories for him, and his heart stopped. He pulled hard on the reins and Apollo reared back in protest. Regaining control of the animal, Darcy leaped off his back. There, on the ground, was a bonnet he remembered. "Elizabeth!"

Frantically, Darcy looked around. He called his wife's name again and listened. There! He sprinted toward the sound, speeding up when he heard a scream get cut short. He crashed through a stand of trees, hearing the panting guards a few feet behind him. As he left the copse, he could see what he most feared: his Elizabeth, limply slung over a man's shoulder. He shouted and the man and his accomplice stopped and looked back. They spoke, but Darcy could not make out the words. Then, Elizabeth was dropped onto the ground and, as Darcy pushed himself to run ever faster, one of the men produced a pistol and aimed it at her head.

With a final burst of speed, Darcy threw himself at the man with the gun. He heard the firearm go off but ignored the sound. Instead, he pinned the shooter to the ground with his hips and began swinging his fists at the man's head. He was dimly aware that the other kidnapper had run, but his focus was on avenging his wife. He had not taken out half his rage when he was pulled off the criminal.

"Sir, stop! You're killing him!"

Two strong arms pulled Darcy back. He fought them at first, but as his mind began to clear of the rage, he remembered Elizabeth and calmed. Shaking the guards off, he instructed them to find some way to restrain both criminals and to send a message to Mr. Smith at the Rose to come with the magistrate. Then, Darcy turned to Elizabeth.

Rushing to her side, Darcy began calling her name, frantically examining her for bullet wounds. His heart leapt into his throat when he felt wetness near her shoulder. He pulled his hand away to find it covered in blood. Moving to her left side, he first tried to pull her spencer away so he could more closely examine the wound, but because she was laying on it, it would only move so far. Swiftly, he untied the bow holding it closed and lifted her a bit, shoving the garment off. Laying Elizabeth on the ground once more, Darcy looked at her joint again, ripping the sleeve of her morning dress to expose the injury.

The wound was bleeding fiercely, or so it appeared to Darcy. He used his clean hand to untie his cravat while pressing his other hand to her shoulder. Soon, his neckcloth was added to the pressure point, but within a short time, it became soaked with blood.

Darcy looked around, frantically searching for assistance. Seeing that the guards had both kidnappers restrained, he called one over. "You there! Yes, you, come here. I need you." Darcy gestured with his free hand. "Hold this tightly," he told the former soldier. "We need more material." Once the guard was in position, Darcy slowly pulled his hand away.

Darcy looked down at himself. The only cloth he had was what he was wearing. A sudden memory flashed in his mind of removing Elizabeth's clothing. *Her petticoat! That will do nicely,"* he thought. With no further ado, Darcy scrambled toward his wife's feet, lifting the hem of her gown. Grasping her petticoat in both hands, he rent the material in two, tearing a wide section off the bottom. The gasp of the guard caught Darcy's attention, and he pulled the gown over her exposed legs.

Folding the piece of petticoat, Darcy knelt beside the guard once more. He could feel the man's horrified stare boring into him. "She is my wife," he snapped, glancing up at the guard.

The former soldier's mouth, which had been hanging open, snapped shut. "Oh," he said before turning his gaze back to Elizabeth and her injury.

It took a few minutes and some maneuvering of the still-unconscious Elizabeth, but soon, her shoulder was bandaged to the best of Darcy's ability. Dismissing his helper with a request for him to go out to the folly and await the others, he gently picked her up, wincing at the bruise forming on the side of her head. He kissed her lips, gently, and whispered in her ear, "Wake up, my love, and tell me you are well."

Shortly thereafter, the third guard came crashing through the trees and into the clearing, Darcy's valet on his heels, along with two other men and the blood-stained guard who had helped Elizabeth. One of the men ran toward the kidnappers, while Smith and the other unknown man ran to Darcy's side.

Dropping onto his knees beside his master, Smith introduced the apothecary.

"This is Mr. Emerson. I thought it best not to alert your aunt's physician just yet."

"Good thinking," Darcy replied. Though he spoke to the valet, his eyes were on Mr. Emerson as he unwrapped the bindings and peeked under the wads of cloth.

"I cannot tell how deep the wound is," the apothecary began as he rewrapped the bandage. "Has she awakened since it happened?" He began to examine the bruise on the side of Elizabeth's head.

"No, she has not." Darcy's reply was terse. His blood still thrummed through his veins and his stomach churned.

Mr. Emerson stood. "We need to move her somewhere so I can extract the bullet, since it seems there was no exit wound."

"I have rented rooms at The Rose. We will take her there." Darcy struggled to his feet with his burden. Smith and the apothecary saw his difficulty and helped him up, then followed as he strode as swiftly as he could manage toward the folly. "Smith," Darcy nodded toward the other side of the field, "I assume that gentleman is the magistrate. Tell him I will speak to him later this afternoon at the inn."

"Yes, sir." Smith bowed and then ran over to relay the message.

By the time Darcy reached the clearing, his valet had caught up again, and he, along with Mr. Emerson, helped Darcy into the carriage with Elizabeth. A few minutes later, as the equipage turned at the parsonage, Darcy remembered Charlotte and called for the driver to stop.

"Smith," Darcy commanded. "Go to the house there and ask for Mrs. Collins. Inform her that I have found Miss Bennet and am taking her to The Rose to be tended by the apothecary. Tell her that time is of the utmost importance, so you cannot explain further, but that I will return later to relate the entire story to her."

With a nod, Smith opened the carriage door and leapt out. Darcy watched as Charlotte opened the door within a few seconds. Her eyes grew wide and her jaw dropped as she listened. Darcy saw her look worriedly at the carriage but nod before closing the door again.

Smith rushed back to the equipage, his mission complete. The door had no more than shut behind him when they were in motion.

At the inn, Darcy disembarked, tersely refusing any assistance that involved him letting go of his wife. He soon had her ensconced in a room hastily prepared by the innkeeper's wife.

Chapter 20

Two hours later, Darcy thanked the apothecary and pressed some coins into his hand. The man had worked diligently to remove the bullet that had lodged in Elizabeth's shoulder and then sew her up. Though Darcy had never before assisted in such a situation, he had a renewed sense of respect for medical men everywhere.

With the apothecary gone, Darcy leaned his arm against the frame of the now-closed door and laid his head on it. His eyes closed and his shoulders slumped, he prayed for what felt like the hundredth time that day for Elizabeth's return to health.

"Mr. Darcy?" Smith stood a respectful distance away, hands clasped before him as he looked at the floor.

Darcy straightened and turned. "Yes?"

"I have taken the liberty of ordering a meal and hot water."

Darcy looked toward the bed, mostly hidden by a screen. "I could use a wash." He turned to Smith and continued, "And a meal. Pull that table to the side of the bed. If Mrs. Darcy awakens in time, I shall attempt to persuade her to eat, as well."

With a bow, the valet turned to do as he was bid. A short while later, Darcy had changed his attire and washed his hands and face. Before he could sit, someone began pounding on the door. "What the-?"

Smith was nearer to the portal than Darcy and reached it first. When he opened it, Mr. Collins stood on the other side.

"I am looking for Mr. Darcy. He has kidnapped my cousin and ruined her reputation, and I insist you tell me where he is."

Smith looked down his nose at the large, heavy gentleman whom he had never seen before. "Mr. Darcy is unavailable." He started to close the door, but the clergyman pushed his way inside.

"Now see here," Collins began, before he caught sight of Darcy standing at the end of the bed. He immediately turned toward that side of the room. "Is that my cousin?" He scurried to the screen but was blocked by Darcy. "Mr. Darcy, what are you doing? You have ruined my cousin by bringing her here. You know an unmarried woman cannot be alone with a gentleman. And, she is in your bed! She has enticed you to do this, I wager. Silly, selfish girl! Oh, what will Lady Catherine say?"

Darcy allowed Collins to dither on for a few more minutes while he debated in his mind how much to tell the rector. Finally deciding that the truth was the best option, he began to speak, cutting Collins off in the middle of a sentence. "Mr. Collins, there is nothing improper about this situation. Miss Elizabeth and I married before I left Scotland. You may leave now, assured in the knowledge that she is Mrs. Darcy and is under my most devoted protection."

Collins stood with jaw hanging and eyes bulging. "But, but ... No, that cannot be. She has lived under my roof as a maiden for nearly a month. Besides, your aunt-"

"My aunt is none of your concern in this matter. She does not know, and you," Darcy paused to bestow upon the rector the stare that intimidated so many people, "will not tell her. It is up to Elizabeth and me to inform our families of our married state when and where we choose. Do you understand me?"

"But-" Collins shrank back as Darcy seemed to grow a foot. "Very well. I do not like this, but very well. I expect you have proof of the marriage?"

"I do," Darcy declared as his brow rose, "but I am not showing it to anyone so wholly unconnected to me."

Collins had opened his mouth while Darcy spoke, intending to impress his outraged opinion further into the gentleman's consciousness, but snapped it shut again at the other man's sharp words. Instead, he bowed and silently walked out the door. As he descended the stairs, the travesty of it all struck him anew and, forgetting that Darcy

203

had charged him to keep it to himself, immediately hastened to Rosings.

Back in the room, Darcy sat on the edge of the bed. Elizabeth had stirred when Collins slammed the door behind him. She opened her eyes as Darcy stroked a gentle hand across her brow. "Fitzwilliam," she croaked.

Darcy smiled. "How good it is to hear your voice, my love. Would you like some water?"

Elizabeth smiled back, turning her face into his hand. "Yes," she whispered. A moment later she was wincing as he helped her to sit and drink. "What happened to me," she moaned as he leaned her back against the pillows that Smith had arranged behind her while she sat up.

"Do you remember anything?" Darcy watched her carefully as he reached for the covered plate of food on the table beside the bed.

A crease appeared above Elizabeth's nose. "I remember leaving the parsonage, I think. I ... I walked to the folly and cried, I missed you so."

Darcy's lips lifted slightly in a tender smile. "I missed you, as well. What else?" He lifted a forkful of beef pie and put it in his mouth.

Elizabeth's eyes darted back and forth as she tried to remember. Suddenly, they grew large. "Someone was there! They grabbed me and dragged me into the trees." She paused, her gaze now focused on Darcy. "I was struck and everything went black, but judging by how much I hurt, I think more must have happened?"

"They did, and yes, more happened." Darcy held the fork toward Elizabeth as he spoke. "Here, have a bite to eat." He nodded approvingly when she accepted the food. "I do not know how much I want to tell you right now, though I suspect you want the entirety of the story immediately, do you not?"

Swallowing, Elizabeth replied, "I would."

Darcy sighed and offered his wife another bite. "Let us do this: I will tell you a little now and the rest on the ride back to London."

The crease between Elizabeth's brows disappeared as they rose nearly to her hairline. "We are going back to London?"

"I should like to. Mr. Collins was just here, and I am certain he is even now rushing into the drawing room at Rosings to tell my aunt that I said we are married, despite the fact that he was told to say nothing. Mr. Emerson left some laudanum for you, and since you have awakened and eaten, I feel comfortable giving you some. It will dull the pain during the trip."

"Oh, my. Well then, I agree with your proposal." Elizabeth took the offered forkful of pie and chewed while Darcy explained that she had been kidnapped and shot.

Elizabeth's eyes grew large again, and she gasped. "Shot? With a gun?" She looked at her arm with its large bandage and her eyes filled up with tears.

Darcy rushed to reassure his wife that it was only a flesh wound, and that she would likely regain full use of her arm, or close to it. He set the plate on the table and pulled her close, taking care not to cause her further physical pain. Then, after her tears had diminished and she was calm again, he insisted she eat more, refusing to say anything else until she had taken the drug left for her and they were in the carriage on the way back to town.

~~~***~~~

Five hours later, the Darcys were home. Elizabeth had been carried in by her husband in front of a scandalized staff and Lord Matlock, who had arrived moments before to leave a message for his nephew. In his most commanding voice, Darcy had instructed everyone—including his uncle—that he would be down presently but for the moment must take care of his wife. That announcement had so shocked his listeners that even Lord Matlock obeyed, allowing him to pass and carry his burden up the stairs.

Smith had arrived in the chamber before his master and, as he had been previously ordered to do, turned down the bed. Now, Darcy laid the half-unconscious Elizabeth in it. He sat beside her and held her hand, then turned to address his valet. "Send bathwater up and send for my physician. I do not know if Elizabeth will wish to eat again when she awakens, but send up a tray with enough for both of us. Go down and tell Mrs. Bishop that I require her assistance and my uncle that if he can wait an hour, I will receive him in the sitting room up here. My mother is not to be allowed admittance for any reason."

"Very good, sir." Smith bowed and retreated through the servant's stairs.

Shortly thereafter, Mrs. Bishop hesitantly knocked on the chamber door. When Darcy let her in, she curtsied. "Smith said you asked for me."

"I did," Darcy replied, gesturing for her to follow him across the room to the fireplace, where he could speak to the housekeeper and still keep an eye on Elizabeth. "I married when in Scotland; we have kept it secret until now, and I expect it to remain that way until I say otherwise." He looked Mrs. Bishop straight in the eye and waited until he had her agreement before he continued. "My wife has been injured; I am awaiting the physician, who has already been sent for. Mrs. Darcy will require a lady's maid. Have you anyone on staff who could take the position?"

"I do. Last quarter-day, I hired the sister of an upstairs maid who had trained as a lady's maid. Her previous employer died in childbed, and she needed a position."

"Very good. You may promote her to be my wife's maid on a trial basis. If Mrs. Darcy likes her, the position will be hers permanently."

"Yes, sir."

"I have already informed Smith, and I am quite certain he passed it on to you, but I wish to make it abundantly clear that my mother is not to be admitted entrance to this suite. The doors to the hallways are to be kept locked at all times. I expect the mistress' chambers to be cleaned and readied for my wife, though for now, she will share everything with me."

"Yes, sir. I will set the maids to it this evening."

"Morning is soon enough, I think. Mrs. Darcy needs her rest and frankly, so do I." Darcy sighed. He was fatigued but wished to get Elizabeth settled before he spoke to his uncle and climbed into the bed beside her. "I want you to attend her for today. I know it will take you away from other duties, and for that, I apologize. It is a measure of my trust in you that I take this step."

"Thank you, sir."

"Come, I will introduce you to her. I will stay to assist you in lifting her when required." With that, Darcy led Mrs. Bishop to the bed and sat on the side of it. "Elizabeth, are you well? Will you wake up for me now?"

Elizabeth's eyes fluttered open at his words, smiling softly at him. "I am relieved to be lying down and still." She ran her tongue over her lips. "Thirsty."

Darcy quickly poured a glass of water from the pitcher beside the bed. He helped her sit up and drink, then settled her back down. "I should imagine you are more comfortable now than you were in the carriage. May I introduce you to your housekeeper, Mrs. Bishop?" He gestured the woman forward. "Mrs. Bishop, this is your new mistress, Mrs. Darcy."

Mrs. Bishop curtseyed. Though shocked at the sight of the lady's bruised face and bloodied gown, the elder lady felt a surge of compassion and motherly feelings for her. "Let us get you washed and changed, shall we? Have you any luggage?"

Elizabeth looked at Darcy, who replied, "There was no time to pack her belongings. For tonight, she may wear one of my nightshirts. I will send to the modiste tomorrow to order her a few items." He stood and walked into the dressing room, asking his valet for the nightshirt.

Soon, Darcy and Mrs. Bishop had Elizabeth washed and changed, and her hair brushed and braided. Mrs. Bishop could see that her new mistress was in pain, and offered a cup of willow bark tea, which Elizabeth gratefully accepted.

When his wife was comfortable, Darcy sent Smith down to let Lord Matlock know that he would be able to speak with him.

Chapter 21

Darcy was waiting by the door that connected the sitting room to his bedchamber when his uncle walked in. He had been keeping an eye on Elizabeth as she rested. Hearing the key turn in the lock and Lord Matlock enter, Darcy pulled the door shut as quietly as he could.

"What is going on, Darcy? You cannot have a woman in your rooms like that!"

"Shut the door, please, Uncle, and lock it. I will explain it all to you." Darcy waited while Matlock did as requested, then he gestured to a seat, silently asking his uncle to sit.

"I can have a woman in my rooms if she is my wife," he began. He held up a hand to silence his uncle, who had begun to exclaim at his words. "I married Miss Elizabeth Bennet in Scotland, at Gretna Green. We have kept the marriage a secret because of my mother. I had hoped to persuade her to accept my wife without more than a bit of argument, but then I found the journal. I was bent on riding to Rosings Saturday night because-."

"You were saving the life of your wife." Matlock sat back in his seat, flabbergasted. He ran a hand over the top of his pomaded hair and gripped the back of his head. "I am speechless. You, who think through every move you make, have married someone you barely know."

"There you are wrong. I met Elizabeth four years ago, in Derbyshire. I had intended to marry her then, the proper way, but Mother would not have it."

Matlock's eyes lit up, and he straightened in his seat as a memory hit him. "That is why her name seemed so familiar! I remember your father talking to me about her and how my sister objected so strongly to her. He bent to Anne's will and sent you away, did he not?"

"He did," Darcy nodded his assent. "He assured me that when my tour was over, he would make certain we wed, if we still wished to, but then he died and I was kept so busy with the estate that I was unable to get to her, though I looked for her everywhere I went."

"And then you found her and did not wish to let her go again." Matlock leaned forward, fascinated by the story of his stoic and staid nephew finding his lost love.

Darcy lifted the corners of his lips in a small but tender smile. "Exactly, and she felt the same. It was as if we had never parted, the feelings were so strong."

Matlock sat back again. "I am interested in all the details—how you hid it from your mother and from Mrs. Darcy's relatives—but I think that should wait. Your mother needs to be dealt with."

Darcy sighed. "She does." He looked down. "I am surprised she has not attempted to force her way in here."

"According to your butler, she has kept to her rooms all day. I saw her at Lord Wycroft's ball last night, and I believe she was rather inebriated. She likely has a bad head today."

Darcy's lips twisted as he continued to stare at his hand where it rested on the ankle that was crossed over his knee. "Celebrating her victory, no doubt." He shook his head. "I feel terrible even thinking that, but it cannot be anything but true." He sighed again and rose, walking to the desk that sat on one side of the room. "I should not have done this, but I asked Smith to search her study downstairs and steal her journal, if he could find it." He picked a book up off the desk and returned to stand beside his uncle's chair, holding the tome out to him. "I looked at enough of it to be certain it is the correct book, but did not look to see if there are any more recent entries than the last one I read."

Matlock at first looked at the journal as though it were a snake that might bite him, but then he inhaled and accepted the diary from Darcy's hand. He opened it and started reading entries, aware that his nephew had seated himself once more and was watching him. When he reached the end, he spoke. "This is worse than I thought it would be." He

213

Zoe Burton

closed the tome and handed it back to Darcy. "I am uncertain what to say, how we should approach this."

Darcy accepted his mother's journal, laying it on the table beside him. He stood. "Would you like some port?"

"Yes, I would, thank you."

Darcy felt his uncle's eyes on his back as he made his way to a cupboard in the corner, pulled out a decanter and two glasses, and poured each of them a drink. He moved deliberately, thinking about Matlock's words and what their options were for dealing with Lady Anne. Moving back to the chairs, Darcy handed a glass to his uncle and sat in his own chair, taking a sip of his port. "As I said when I spoke to you last, sending Mother to Bedlam is not a choice. It will do none of us any good."

"No, it will not. So, you are left with installing her at the dower house or sending her to Scotland, to Glenmoor." Matlock tilted his head, examining Darcy. "After what she has done, the injury she has caused, I cannot imagine you want her at Pemberley."

Darcy snorted. "Frankly, no, but I also think I may wish for her to be somewhere I can keep watch on her. Neither do I feel that Glenmoor is a wise choice; she has friends there." He paused as an idea took root. "There is a small estate in Cheshire that my father purchased about a year before he passed away, called Black Hall. It has a Tudor monstrosity of a house and is isolated. The nearest estate is thirty miles away, and the closest town is ten. If we are to punish her, we must send her to a place where she has no connections."

Matlock nodded. "I agree." He hesitated, then spoke again. "Here is a thought; feel free to set me straight if you must." He waited for Darcy to look at him. "This may be out of our hands. I assume the magistrate has spoken to you. Will there be charges filed against my sister?"

"No, we are to be spared that. The kidnappers were all too eager, once they arrived at the jail, to explain who had hired them. The one who shot Elizabeth appears to be the ringleader. He did not have Mother's name, thankfully. He only knew that a fine lady in London had hired him. No one was killed, and the magistrate thought it would not do for a gentlewoman's reputation to be ruined, meaning Elizabeth's." Darcy shook his head. "The men will be charged with attacking me and the guards I hired and nothing else."

"That is enough to get Newgate for a few years." Matlock spoke thoughtfully. "They could use this in the future to blackmail you and your wife."

"I doubt that. I beat the leader so badly he will not be recognizable for a good long while, and neither knows who I am." Darcy felt his chest rise as it filled with a feeling of satisfaction that could only be described as savage.

"Oh." Lord Matlock's brows rose, but he said nothing further.

"Regardless, the matter is neatly tied up with little effort from any of us. The kidnappers could somehow get out of prison, examine their facts and ask around, discovering Mother's name in the process, but who would they know with connections enough to us be able to tell them?" Darcy shook his head again, taking another sip of his beverage.

"True. That is a blessing, I think." Matlock paused and gazed at his nephew, who was currently staring into the empty fireplace. "Well, then. We are back to our decision: Pemberley's dower house or this estate in Cheshire? In either case, servants can be hired that will not bend to Anne's will, and you can receive regular reports. You will be in charge of her money, I can make that so myself if you have any difficulty with the bankers."

"If I send her to Black Hall …," Darcy sighed. "I will worry about the servants, no matter where I send her. She has a propensity to beat them, and I cannot allow it."

"We must make clear to her what her choices are and what the consequences will be for things such as that. To be honest, knowing my sister's enjoyment of money and society, I think being banished to somewhere far from London without a penny to spend will break her, especially with no other families near. I hate to say it, but there it is."

Darcy's eyes moved from the fireplace to his uncle. "We are taught in church to honour our parents. We are to respect them and help them and do things for them. I struggle with the feeling that sending Mother away is the opposite of that."

"No, Darcy," Matlock replied, "it is not. You are honouring her; you are providing her with food, shelter, and clothing. She is still responsible for her own actions. She has never been checked the way she should have been. Oh, your father did, to an extent, but too often, he gave in. I understand why he did, but he should not have. Now it falls to you to do what he should have had the courage to do long ago."

With a sigh, Darcy stood. "Well, then, that is what I shall do. She will go to Cheshire. I will hire the most severe servants I can find, and she will live out her days in exile." He looked at the door as if he could see through it to the precious treasure on the other side. "I hate to leave Elizabeth right now, but do not wish to expose her to Mother any further."

Matlock stood to stand alongside his nephew. "I will go and act as your agent. Audra can come with us."

Darcy nodded again. "Thank you. I appreciate the offer." He looked at the door to the hallway. "We need to confront her. When do you want to do it?"

"It will take time to set the trip up, but we can confront her now. Better to get it over with tonight than to cause upset to the household."

"Very well, then, let us speak to her immediately." Darcy pulled the door open and marched into the hall, Lord Matlock following closely behind. Arriving at Lady Anne's room, he knocked and waited. After a minute or two of insisting to his mother's maid that he be allowed in, Darcy pushed his way past her.

"What is this?" Lady Anne, prepared to go out, stood in front of her dressing table. "I told Ruth to inform you that I am unavailable."

Chapter 22

"Sit down, Mother. Uncle and I are here to discuss something with you." Darcy wore his mask; his face was set in stone, its expression blank. Only his eyes, with their intense stare, and the flush to his skin gave away his hurt and anger.

"I think not, Fitzwilliam! I-." Lady Anne's voice was cut off by her brother's louder one.

"It was not a request, Sister. Sit down now." Lord Matlock stepped toward Lady Anne, a thunderous frown creasing the skin between his heavy, black brows.

Lady Anne's eyes grew wide, and she pulled back from her brother, dropping onto the stool behind her. Her eyes darted back and forth between her son and Matlock. When Darcy began to speak, she focused on him.

Taking a deep breath, Darcy braced himself and then began. "When I was in Scotland, I found something that belongs to you. I was horrified by what it contained."

Lord Matlock held his sister's journal up. He had grabbed it off the table in Darcy's sitting room as he walked past it. "Does this look familiar to you?"

Lady Anne had just begun to gather her thoughts after the unprecedented interaction she had just had with her brother. Now, those words flew out of her head again as she recognized the book he was holding. "How did you get that?" She stood suddenly, darting toward her brother with hands outstretched. He held it up and out of her reach, instantly glowering at her as he had before and instructing her to sit back down. Lady Anne clenched her jaw and ground her teeth, clearly desiring to put him in his place. She did not, however. Before he could tell her another time, she stepped back and seated herself once more.

"Clearly, it *is* familiar." Matlock's lip curled. "What a monster you are. Mother would be turning in her grave if she knew what you have been up to."

"Do not speak about Mother to me," Lady Anne demanded.

Darcy chose to interrupt so as to prevent the conversation from wandering away from the topic at hand. "What have you to say about the contents?"

Snapping her head towards her son, Lady Anne spat, "I have nothing to say about them. What I wrote is none of your concern, and I am ashamed that a child of mine could be so rude as to read a person's private words."

"Enough, Mother!" Darcy's anger pounded in his blood. His vision narrowed until he was no longer aware of his uncle being in the room, nor of his wife, sleeping down the hall. "I know what I read; tales of the beatings of servants and poisoning of others who went against your will. You murdered your own husband. Your *husband*, who loved you completely, and who you swore you loved in return."

"He deserved it! He told that Bennet chit that he would make certain she married you after your tour. You were sent away to remove you from her presence. It was not my will for you to marry the likes of her. Now, you will be rid of her forever and will marry a lady of my choosing." It was Lady Anne's turn to sneer, and her lip curled at the thought of Elizabeth Bennet lying dead in a field.

Now Darcy stepped forward, stopping directly in front of his mother. "That is what you think, Mother. Elizabeth lives, and she lies sleeping in the master's suite. I rescued her from your hired killer just this morning."

Lady Anne's smirk turned into a frown while the crease between her brows made another appearance. "What?" she shrieked, leaping to her feet again.

"You heard me." Darcy's voice turned from angry to cold as he stepped back. "Uncle Matlock will be taking you to one of the estates Father purchased before he died, in Cheshire, where you will live out your years. I

221

will control your funds, as well as who may visit and who may not and who works in the household. You are no longer welcome in my homes." Darcy glared at his mother once more, then sketched a shallow bow to his uncle and turned away, leaving the room with a quiet click of the door latch. He returned to the master's chambers, entering from the sitting room he had so recently vacated.

~~~***~~~

The next morning, Darcy awoke curled around Elizabeth. He smiled, nuzzling her hair. After a few minutes of cuddling her close, he lifted up on one arm, his elbow bent, meaning to kiss her forehead before he crawled out of bed. He was surprised to see Elizabeth's eyes open.

"You are awake." Instead of her head, Darcy kissed Elizabeth's lips.

"I am. I woke a little while ago. I have been laying here with my eyes closed, listening to the sounds." Elizabeth's lips lifted a little, into a wan smile.

"I would imagine from the look on your face that you are also trying to lie still, because you are in pain." Darcy stroked his wife's cheek.

"That, too," Elizabeth admitted, flashing her smile once more.

"Let me ring Mrs. Bishop and get you more of that willow bark tea."

"Thank you, Fitzwilliam." Elizabeth blushed but bravely asked the question that had been growing in her mind while she waited for him to awaken. "Will you help me to the chamber pot?"

"I will." Darcy kissed her, then dashed around the bed to assist Elizabeth up. Once she was seated behind the screen in the dressing room, he rang the bell, giving the housekeeper instructions to bring up breakfast and the willow tea. Then, he helped Elizabeth back to bed and got in beside her, holding her close. While they waited for their meal, Darcy relayed the conversations he had with his uncle and mother the night before.

"I have to admit that I am relieved," Elizabeth said. "Knowing those scoundrels were hired by Lady Anne, and that they intended to kill me, makes me leery of her. I will feel much better knowing she is far away, as long as she stays away."

"She will not have the use of a carriage or horses, and will not be allowed to leave the estate. My uncle will stand as my proxy in the hiring of new servants, ones who will strictly follow the rules I lay down." Darcy kissed Elizabeth's head before laying his cheek on it. The two fell silent then, holding each other close, until the housekeeper knocked on the door.

Shortly thereafter, Darcy shut the door behind the servants and arranged the meal on the bed, where they could reach everything. Then, he carefully climbed up to sit beside his wife.

"It is like a picnic. A picnic in bed," Elizabeth giggled.

Darcy laughed with her, and then pulled the covers off the two plates and took turns eating his food and feeding Elizabeth hers. When she could take no more and had emptied her cup of willow bark tea, Darcy put the remains of the meal back on the table beside the bed and tucked his wife back in. "Sleep now," he urged, kissing her and smoothing the hair off her face. "I love you." He sat beside her until she fell into a light sleep. Then, he rose and went down to his study to write some letters.

~~~***~~~

An hour or so later, Darcy ascended the staircase and entered his rooms again. Elizabeth still slept, so he took the book that had been sitting on the seat of a chair by the window and settled in to read for an hour or two, only putting the volume of Shakespeare away when his wife began to stir. Once he determined that she would appreciate a bath and a change of clothes, he rang for Smith, asking for bathwater and for the maid who had been assigned to Elizabeth.

Before long, a very much refreshed Elizabeth was ensconced in a chair, a stool under her feet and another of Darcy's clean nightshirts covering her curves. She was covered from neck to toes with a blanket, because Smith was changing the sheets on the bed.

"My personal physician tended you last evening, but I do not know if you will recall it. You slept through the majority of his examination." Darcy watched Elizabeth carefully. A second cup of tea had eased the lines of strain around her mouth, but it was clear she did not feel at all well.

Brows knit, Elizabeth shook her head. "I am afraid I do not remember. What was his evaluation of my case?"

"He said the stitches were among the best he had seen in all his years. He will return this evening but said that as long as infection does not set in, you will be well. You may have some problems with movement even after it heals, but there is no way to determine that for a surety."

"I am happy to hear Mr. Emerson's work is so well accepted." Elizabeth yawned. "I can see that your valet has the bed almost covered again, and once I get in it, I will probably fall asleep quickly, so let us discuss my aunt and uncle while I am still awake."

"We need to tell them of our marriage."

"We do, and I would rather not wait." Elizabeth yawned again, sending yearning glances toward the bed.

"No, I would not, either. While you are asleep, I will send a note 'round to the earl. I am certain he has hired footmen to keep my mother inside her chambers until she leaves for Glenmoor, but I would like to be assured of it without leaving your side to walk down the hall and look." When he saw Elizabeth's brow rise and her gaze turn to Smith, he added, "I prefer the servants not be involved any more than they already are."

Elizabeth nodded. "I understand. Is there a way we can get the Gardiners here without Lady Anne discovering it?"

"If you were healthy enough to go downstairs, I would not hesitate. However, the only option, until you are, is for the Gardiners to come up here, to our sitting room." Darcy thought for a few minutes, his eyes still sharply watching his wife. "Let me send this missive. I believe that if she is restricted to her rooms, there should be no problem."

Elizabeth smiled. "Thank you, love."

"Anything for you," Darcy replied, kissing her head before walking into the sitting room.

Chapter 23

Darcy's uncle replied to his note immediately. Lady Anne was well-guarded and
would not be able to do anything but fume in
her rooms if she did not like what was happening in other areas of the house. With that
in mind, Darcy wrote a note to the Gardiners,
asking them to visit Darcy House today, if
they could and informing them that Elizabeth
was with him. He sent it to Gracechurch
Street in the hands of one of the grooms, who
was told to wait for a reply before he returned.
Then, Darcy gathered his correspondence and
the household accounts and took them upstairs so he could work on them while watching over Elizabeth.

By the time he had gone over the accounts, the messenger had returned. Darcy
handed the boy a shilling and sent him back
to the stables, closing the door behind him.
He broke the seal on the letter in his hand as
he turned, unfolding the note while walking
toward the bed. He sat on the edge of the mat-
tress to read.

"What does it say?" Elizabeth's voice
was still sleepy after her recent nap.

"He and your aunt will follow this note by no less than an hour." Darcy smiled when Elizabeth cried, "Oh, good!"

"Will you help me up? I need something to wear. I cannot greet my aunt and uncle in your nightshirt." Elizabeth threw back the covers with her good hand, groaning when the action pulled on the stitches in the opposite shoulder. "You would not think this side would hurt when it was the other I used," she grumbled.

"They are all connected, as you well know, or should," Darcy scolded as he helped her sit up and turn to dangle her legs off the edge of the bed. "You are supposed to be taking it easy and allowing me to help you."

Elizabeth groaned again. "I know, I know. I am sorry." She clutched his hand and waited for the wave of pain to diminish.

When Darcy felt her begin to relax again, he assured her that she would be able to change her clothes. "I had your new maid go through my sister's closet. Georgiana is about your height, though she is on a bit larger scale. Jenny found a few gowns she thought might do for you for now."

"Oh, good," Elizabeth sighed. "It will feel wonderful to be dressed like a normal person again."

"I have no doubt," Darcy chuckled. He reached over and rang the bell, and when Smith appeared, asked him to send Jenny in.

When the maid arrived, Darcy helped his wife into her dressing room and left her in the maid's capable hands.

Darcy was just entering the room after returning the books and letters to his study when Jenny assisted Elizabeth into the bed-chamber, dressed and with her hair done up in an elegant style. Darcy's heart skipped a beat, and he stopped to drink in the sight.

Jenny smiled and curtseyed before silently leaving the couple alone.

"What is wrong?" Elizabeth began fussing with the piece of silk she and Jenny had fashioned into a sling to hold her arm still.

"Nothing is wrong," Darcy replied, moving toward her again. He stopped in front of her and reached for her hand, bringing it to his lips to kiss before leaning down to her ear and whispering, "You take my breath away." He caressed her ear with his lips, then kissed her cheek and finally her mouth.

Elizabeth sighed. "You take mine, as well. Kiss me again." She blushed as she realized what she had said, but Darcy's laugh told her he enjoyed her impulsiveness.

"Your wish is my command," Darcy teased before kissing her breathless.

Several minutes later, they separated. Darcy grinned at his wife's dazed look. "Come, my love," he said. "Your family should be here soon."

Elizabeth cleared her throat as she accepted Darcy's assistance. Once on her feet with her good hand tucked under his elbow, she replied, "Indeed," and allowed him to lead her next door to the sitting room.

They had no more than settled on the settee when the Gardiners were announced. Elizabeth stood once more, with Darcy's help. "Aunt, Uncle," she exclaimed. "How good it is to see you!"

Maddie rushed to Elizabeth's side, wrapping her in a careful hug. "What has happened to you? Why are you here and not in Kent?"

"I am wondering about that also," Gardiner said, turning his narrow-eyed gaze in Darcy's direction. "If I did not trust my ability to judge characters, I would have called you out already."

Darcy bowed, his manners leading him as always. "Please, have a seat. We will be happy to explain."

When they were all seated, Darcy and Elizabeth looked at each other. They had agreed that Darcy would take the lead in the explanations, and when Elizabeth gave him a small nod, he took a deep breath and began.

"First, we have a confession to make. Elizabeth and I married at a church in Gretna Green the night before the Reids' ball." The mouths of the Gardiners fell open in the same manner at the same time. Darcy heard Elizabeth's slight cough and knew she was amused, but he was far too nervous to be so frivolous. He rushed onward before his guests gathered their thoughts. "We decided to keep it secret for a few weeks because we knew my mother would cause trouble. We hoped to persuade her to accept it, and then we would make a public announcement."

Gardiner was the first to regain his composure. "Since this is the first we have heard of a marriage, and there has been no public announcement, I take it you were unsuccessful." His voice had a hard edge. It was clear that he was displeased with the situation.

"No, but we never had an opportunity to try. Two nights before you left Scotland, I found her diary." Darcy went on to explain what the journal had contained.

"That was the reason for the armed footmen that travelled with us," Maddie exclaimed, her hand on her heart.

"It was," Darcy conceded. "If you had not accepted, they would still have accompanied you, but at a distance."

"I thank you for that. Though we did not know the danger we were in, it did make for a less worrisome trip." Gardiner sat back in his chair, arms crossed. "Elizabeth made it to Kent in perfect health, yet now she sits here with an injury."

"My mother discovered our marriage. She hired someone to kill Elizabeth." Darcy

Zoe Burton

paused for a few seconds when Maddie gasped
and covered her mouth. When nothing else
was said, he continued, "Thankfully, my uncle
has a man in my household who reports to
him the goings-on in regards to my mother,
and he alerted me. I had hired some former
soldiers to guard Elizabeth before I left Kent
and they were with me when I rescued her
from the kidnappers' clutches. They are currently being held in the jail at Hunsford village. I brought Elizabeth here after the apothecary had treated her." Darcy explained the
injuries Elizabeth had received, though they
could clearly see the bruise on the side of her
head.

"Oh, Lizzy, that must have been a miserable ride," Maddie exclaimed. "However did
you do it?"

"Mr. Emerson had given me a mild dose of
laudanum. I was half-asleep most of the time."

"Mr. Darcy," Gardiner began, then
sighed. "I do not know what to say. I am unhappy at being deceived, but you did save my
niece's life, and for that I am thankful. You
should have told us that you had married." He
held up a hand when Elizabeth began to protest. "I know your reasons and I understand
them, but I have failed in my duty to you, and
that does not sit well with me. Your father will
be furious with me."

"I would hope that Papa would forgive
you once he hears the story," Elizabeth re-

marked. "We will tell him ourselves, and absolve you of all culpability." She looked at Darcy.

"Indeed, we will. It is my responsibility now as Elizabeth's husband to take care of it. We have freely admitted that we went behind your back, eloping in the night."

Gardiner shook his head. "You may do as you please, but I will not shirk my duty in this. I will ride out there tomorrow and tell him."

"Perhaps," Maddie interjected, "you would deliver messages from Lizzy and Darcy? Reading the news in his daughter's own hand might soften the blow." She looked at her niece and new nephew. "If you were well enough, Lizzy, I would insist you go with your uncle, but that would be foolish at this time, and I daresay Darcy would refuse to allow you to go if I did." She grinned at Darcy, who had begun shaking his head.

"You are undoubtedly correct, Aunt," Elizabeth declared with a soft laugh. She looked at her husband and reached her free hand out to lay atop his. "I would have him no other way."

"You say that now," Gardiner said, "but the first time he becomes protective when you are well, you will change your mind." His voice dripped sarcasm, and the ladies in the room laughed.

"Poor Edward," Maddie teased. "So put-upon by your independent-minded wife." She laughed again when her husband rolled his eyes.

After visiting a few minutes longer and getting Darcy's assurance that he would send a messenger later that day with letters for Mr. Bennet, the Gardiners left. Darcy assisted Elizabeth across the room and into the bed-chamber, tucking her back into bed for a much-needed rest.

Chapter 24

Three days later, the notice of their marriage was printed in the paper. Darcy brought it to Elizabeth in their sitting room. She had refused to remain prone in bed for the weeks it would take her arm to heal. Darcy reluctantly agreed to her scheme as long as she promised she would stay seated and rest when her body required it.

"Look, love, at what is in the paper this morning." Darcy handed her the newssheet, pointing to the correct place.

Elizabeth took the paper, her face lighting up to see her name linked to his and began to read the announcement aloud. "Mr. Fitzwilliam Darcy of Pemberley, Derbyshire and Darcy House, London, announces his marriage to Miss Elizabeth Bennet of Longbourn in Hertfordshire." She grinned at the newssheet, then up at her husband. "How well that looks!"

Darcy returned Elizabeth's smile. "Indeed, it does." He leaned down and kissed her, then seated himself on the settee, moving her skirts out of the way before he lowered his frame to the cushion. "I have more news."

Zoe Burton

Elizabeth's attention was pulled from the paper. She tilted her head at her husband. "Your mother is gone?"

Darcy nodded. "She is. They left at dawn. Uncle left a note for me."

"I thought I heard movement in the hallways in the wee hours." Elizabeth sighed. "I am still a bit uneasy. There is no real way to control her actions, no matter where she is."

Darcy rubbed his hand over Elizabeth's lower leg, which rested beside his thigh. "We must trust in the safeguards my uncle is putting into place and the isolation of the estate she will reside in. All will be well."

Elizabeth lifted a single eyebrow. "Indeed."

Darcy tilted his head to the side and then back up. He turned his attention to the post in his hand. Sorting through it, he held one up. "This is from Longbourn."

"Really?" Elizabeth sat up straight, reaching for the missive. "Oh, it is from Papa!" She quickly snapped the seal and unfolded the note, turning it so it was right side up. She read it through and then went to the top and began again. When she got to the bottom, she lowered the note to her lap and bit her lip.

"Is it bad?" A crease had formed between Darcy's brows as he observed her.

"He expresses his disappointment with my choices and his concern over my future happiness. He has neither forgotten nor forgiven your mother for her long-ago actions, I fear." Elizabeth glanced up at Darcy for a moment, but then looked back down at her letter. "He extends his best wishes and my mother's effusions at such a good catch for one of her daughters. He asks that I keep him apprised of our movements, so that he may surprise us with a visit in the future."

Darcy wrapped his arm around Elizabeth's shoulders, being careful not to touch her injury. "You will, of course. Your family is always welcome here."

Elizabeth tilted her head at him, her eyes narrowed. "I seem to recall a certain lack of enthusiasm for that four years ago."

Darcy blushed, but countered her argument. "I have learned a great deal in the intervening time. I love you," he continued somberly, "and if having you means having your mother also, then I will welcome her with open arms." He leaned toward kiss his wife. "Your mouth is hanging open, Wife. Is that an invitation?" Before she could respond, his lips covered hers.

Elizabeth swiftly recovered from her surprise and was an active participant in the breathtaking kiss, even going so far as to wrap the hand of her uninjured arm around his neck, bringing him closer.

~~~***~~~

A fortnight passed, and Elizabeth had healed enough that she was comfortable being seen in the public rooms of the house. The bruising had faded to a pale yellow that was easily covered with face powder. She still made use of a sling for her arm, though the physician had been in the day before to remove her stitches, a process that she hoped fervently that she never had to experience again.

Darcy remained insistent that his wife rest as much as she could, and though she fought him on it more now that she was feeling better, he was still able to carry his point more often than not. Darcy knew that once her arm had regained its strength and her occasional headaches had passed into memory, it would be much harder to persuade her to his way of thinking and behaving. He worried most about Elizabeth's enjoyment of daily walking. He would not restrict her movements, but he would take measures to protect her. The memory of her lying, so still and pale, in that field at Rosings haunted him.

"Mr. Darcy?" The butler paused in the open doorway of Darcy's study, the silver salver designated for the post held in front of him.

Darcy looked up and, seeing who it was, waved the servant in. He accepted the mail and sent the butler away after ascertaining that there was nothing else the man required. He automatically began sorting the letters into piles when an envelope bordered in black caught his eye. He set it to the side for the time it took to sort the rest, then picked the note up again. "This is postmarked Cheshire," he murmured. Breaking the seal, he began to read. His eyes widened and his mouth fell open. "I cannot believe it," he cried.

Rising, the letter held in one hand, Darcy began to pace the room, his free hand lifting to run through his hair. "Oh, my word." He sank onto the chair beside the fireplace. "I must tell Elizabeth." With those words, he rose and strode down the hall to the sitting room.

Elizabeth heard Darcy enter the room and lowered her embroidery hoop to her lap. She started to see his hair disheveled and a look of sorrow in his eyes. "What has happened?"

Darcy slumped into the seat beside her. He opened his mouth once to speak but shut it again, as if struggling for words. Finally, he heaved a great sigh and said, "This letter," he waved it a bit and then lowered it to his lap once more, "is from Lord Matlock. My mother is dead."

Elizabeth gasped, bringing her hand to her mouth. "How? I cannot believe it!" She let go of her hoop and reached for the missive, skimming it as she listened to Darcy's explanation.

"He does not know, he says. She argued and fought with him all the way to Black Hall, and for the first two days they were there. She spent the next two pouting, refusing to speak to him at all. The following day, she was found dead in the gardens."

"He says there were no visible injuries and no signs of poison." Elizabeth looked up. "Given her history, I am glad he looked into that possibility." She handed the letter back.

Darcy lifted his brows and nodded. "I, as well." He accepted the note, folding it back up. "He said he would take her to Matlock and bury her there. The funeral could be over by now."

"It could," Elizabeth agreed, "but I think we should go, regardless. You will want to pay your last respects to her, even though you did not get on well."

Darcy signed deeply, looking at the floor. "I will, yes. We will need mourning clothes made up for you, for I will not go without you. My mother will wait for her due." He looked up at his wife. "Does it make me a bad person that I feel more relief than sadness at her passing?"

Elizabeth shook her head. "No, it does not. Your relationship with your mother was not what it should have been, but that was due to her actions, not yours. You did your duty to her by providing a home for her after your father passed, and by keeping her name out of the scandal sheets when you discovered her horrifying crimes. She made your life difficult, thereby making herself difficult to love." Elizabeth grasped one of Darcy's hands. "If you are a bad person, then I am too, for I could shout with joy that I do not have to live in fear of her making an escape or hiring a cutthroat to kill me."

Darcy lifted the corners of his lips into a small smile. "I see your point. I am sad that Mother has died, and that we could not be the mother and son I wanted us to be, but if I am honest, I feel the same as you. I will not allow guilt or any other emotion to eat at me about this. Mother made her choices, and whatever or whoever killed her matters not. She is gone, and we have our entire lives to live together." He pulled the hand that was held by Elizabeth's to his mouth to bestow a kiss upon it.

"We shall have quite the tale to tell our children one day about our secret marriage." Elizabeth's mien took on the mischievous look it always did when she teased.

Darcy laughed. "That, we shall!"

The Darcys travelled to Pemberley a few days later. They remained quietly at home for half a year, missing out on the social season entirely, which neither of them minded in the least. Happily free from danger, they settled into the business of building a loving and strong marriage.

The End

Before you go ...

If you enjoyed this book, please consider leaving a review at the store where you purchased it.

Also, consider joining my mailing list at the URL below to receive updates about my books, free books, and more.

https://mailchi.mp/ee42ccbc6409/zoeburtonsignup

~Zoe

About the Author

Zoe Burton first fell in love with Jane Austen's books in 2010, after seeing the 2005 version of Pride and Prejudice on television. While making her purchases of Miss Austen's novels, she discovered Jane Austen Fan Fiction; soon after that she found websites full of JAFF. Her life has never been the same. She began writing her own stories when she ran out of new ones to read.

Zoe lives in a 100-plus-year-old house in the snow-belt of Ohio with her two Boxers. She is a former Special Education Teacher, and has a passion for romance in general, Pride and Prejudice in particular, and NASCAR.

Zoe belongs to the Jane Austen Society of North America, and JASNA's Ohio North Coast chapter.

Connect with Zoe Burton

Email:
zoe@zoeburton.com

Twitter:
https://twitter.com/ZoeBurtonAuthor

Facebook:
https://www.facebook.com/ZoeBurtonBooks
https://www.facebook.com/groups/BurtonsBabes/

MeWe:
https://mewe.com/i/zoe.burton

Pinterest:
https://www.pinterest.com/zoeburtonauthor/

Instagram:
https://www.instagram.com/zoeburtonauthor/

Website:
https://zoeburton.com

Join my mailing list:
https://mailchi.mp/ee42ccbc6409/zoeburtonsignup

Support me at Patreon:
https://www.patreon.com/zoeburtonauthor

Me at Austen Authors:
http://austenauthors.net/zoe-burton/

More by Zoe Burton

Regency Single Titles:

I Promise To...

Lilacs & Lavender

Promises Kept

Bits of Ribbon and Lace (Short Stories-available exclusively to newsletter subscribers)

Decisions and Consequences

Mr. Darcy's Love

Darcy's Deal

The Essence of Love

Matches Made at Netherfield

Darcy's Perfect Present

Darcy's Surprise Betrothal

To Save Elizabeth

Darcy Overhears

Merry Christmas, Mr. Darcy!

Westerns:

Darcy's Bodie Mine

Bundles:

Darcy's Adventures

Forced to Wed

Promises

Mr. Darcy Finds Love (available exclusively to
newsletter subscribers)

The Darcy Marriage Series Books 1-3

Mr. Darcy, My Hero

The Darcy Marriage Series:

Darcy's Wife Search

Lady Catherine Impedes

Caroline's Censure

Contemporary Settings:

Darcy's Race to Love

Georgie's Redemption